SUGAR ENEMY

SUGAR DADDIES #10

CHARITY PARKERSON

--Warning: This book is intended for readers over the age of 18.

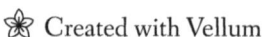 Created with Vellum

INTRODUCTION

AFTER MONTHS OF PUSH AND PULL, LAW AND COY ARE THE LINE BETWEEN LOVE AND HATE.

Since the day David brought Coy home, black and blue and in need of protection, Law has felt more than he should. Coy always takes him through every emotion. Law doesn't want to want Coy. Coy is as dramatic as he is beautiful. He's also the angriest person Law has ever met. Law is too old to deal with a sexy, young mess. He can't stop.

It seemed the second Coy found himself working for Law, nothing he did was good enough. No matter how hard he tries, Law finds him lacking. That doesn't explain why Law looks at him like no one ever has or why Coy burns for Law's touch. Most of all, Law makes him feel safe. Not only is that something Coy has never experienced, it's something he needs, because Coy is a magnet for the damaged.

As crazy as Coy might make Law, Coy is his. No one touches Coy. Looks at Coy. Steals Coy from him. Unless he doesn't step up his game, that is.

ONE

THIS BOOK HAS ALL THE TRIGGERS.

TWO

Coy: *I HAVE A CODE RED EMERGENCY. LAW HAS A date, and obviously, it's not with me.*

Jonah: *Oh no. How did you find this out?*

Coy: *During his usual berating session. He told me I needed to try harder to get done on time today, because he has a date, and he wouldn't be late because I'm dragging my feet.*

Jonah: *Damn.*

Coy: *Yeah.*

Jonah: *Well, obviously, you'll have to go out tonight too. You can't sit home while he goes out, or he wins.*

Coy's throat swelled as he read Jonah's text. Law had a date. Never in the history of ever had one piece of knowledge cut Coy as deeply. All day, Coy had switched between anger, hurt, and telling himself he didn't care. Every time he set eyes on Law, he knew that last one was a lie. The thing was, he shouldn't care. Nine months ago, David Baker, the owner of the ranch where he currently lived and worked, had saved Coy. Coy had been trapped in an ugly, abusive relationship. All hope of escaping had bled from him, and then Coy had landed in the hospital. Left with no one else to call, Coy had contacted his ex, Tyrone. Except Tyrone hadn't shown up alone. He'd brought along his man, David. Even at his lowest, Coy hadn't wanted to accept David's help. David wouldn't be moved. So Coy had landed here, living and working every day alongside Law... It was a nightmare.

Lawson Yates was nearly twenty years older than Coy. He was also six-foot-two and solid muscle. Law had gorgeous dark skin and a wicked smile. His brown eyes were so light they were almost honey-colored. From day one, Law seemed dedicated to humbling Coy. He spent more hours of the day following Coy and browbeating him than Law spent running the place. Baker Ranch ran smoothly. As the property manager and all-around boss, Law was obviously good at his job. Unfortunately, he was so good at it, he obviously had tons of free time to torment Coy. The time Law didn't dedicate to working and berating Coy, he spent watching Coy in a way that took Coy's breath. Coy hated himself for feeling anything other than animosity toward Law. Of course, that was Coy's biggest flaw. He always fell for men who left him mentally or physically scarred. Coy's only saving grace was that Law didn't know Coy craved his touch. Only one person knew that shameful secret, Coy's friend Jonah.

Jonah was another gift David had given him. He was close to Coy's age and newly married. Jonah was solid and sweet. He thought of David as a father and David loved Jonah like a son. After one conversation, Jonah had won Coy's friendship for life. Jonah kept him sane. That was exactly what Coy needed now.

Coy cast a quick look around the stables. All the horses were out in the field, getting their exercise and soaking up the sun. Law had disappeared while Coy had been trying not to look at him. Now everything was quiet. These moments were his favorite and the reason he kept working for David. The scent of fresh hay filled the warm air. Different animal sounds carried on the light breeze blowing through the open barn doors. This place, it was peaceful. It was exactly what Coy needed. Today, with the news of Law's upcoming date choking him, nothing brought him peace.

Coy's phone buzzed. Before he could check Jonah's latest message, voices moved in his direction. Coy cast a glance around, looking for a quick place to hide. He slipped inside the closest empty stall. David didn't care how many calls and texts Coy sent while on the clock. David wasn't who Coy hoped to avoid. Coy snagged an empty bucket and sat. This place was all he had. At one time, Coy had been at the clubs and meeting new people. He went out every weekend and knew someone at every hot spot. Now he had nothing but this ranch and the comfort it brought to his life. Well, he also had Jonah. Coy opened his messages.

Jonah: *Leave everything to me. John says we'll pick you up at eight.*

This was why he loved Jonah. No matter how low he felt or how ridiculous his problems must seem, Jonah always came through.

Coy: *Thank you. I'll see you at eight.*

"Are you being fucking serious right now?"

Coy's chin jerked up at the yelled words. Law stood feet away, staring at him over the edge of the stall door. His sexy honey eyes were narrowed on Coy.

Coy's temper snapped. No one got under his skin like Law. "I'm done for the day," Coy growled, pushing to his feet. "I'm allowed some privacy." He shoved the door open, forcing Law to step back. He needed away from Law. He couldn't look at the man right now, knowing he was a few short hours away from touching someone else. That didn't mean Coy could stop his tongue from trying to get in one last dig. "You don't have to worry about me fucking up your date the way I fuck up your whole day."

Law's hand shot out, snagging Coy's arm, stopping him from getting away. Before Coy had time for the usual spurt of fear that always came with being manhandled, Law's thumb caressed him. That one small touch was all it took to hold Coy captive and ease his fears. His gaze shot to Law's face. The hint of something that kept Coy hoping was back. Law held his stare. "I never accused you of fucking up anything. Don't run off thinking that."

Coy licked his suddenly dry lips. His gaze dropped to Law's full bottom lip without thought. The air changed, filling with electricity. "What should I think?"

Law dropped Coy's arm. Coy's gaze snapped back to Law's. There was heat in Law's eyes. Coy didn't think he was imagining things. Law felt the same spark. "You should think about going out. You should be spending time with people your age."

A smile that felt faked even to Coy pulled at his lips. As unnatural as the gesture felt, Coy knew his smile had to look it too. "No worries in that department. I won't be alone tonight."

Law looked away. "That's good. You should get lost, then. I'm sure it'll take time to get your hair just right."

At Law's bitchy tone, an evil smile slowly spread across Coy's face. If Law wanted to fight, he'd come to the right place. Coy had been pissed all day and looking for an excuse. "There's no rush. Us young people don't go out until late. You should head out, though. I'd hate for you to miss your chance to combine your senior citizen discount with the early bird special."

7

Humor filled Law's eyes, but he didn't smile. "I'm not worried over that. When people get to be my age, they don't expect to be fed before they're fucked."

Coy refused to flinch. Hell would freeze before he ever let Law know how deep he cut. "Then I should definitely get out of your hair," Coy said, amazing even himself with how unaffected he sounded. "Or lack thereof," he added, casting a glance toward the head Law kept shaved bald. "Your date shouldn't have to endure you showing up late *and* disappointing them in the same night."

"Not all of us are as well rested from doing nothing all day, as you are," Law shot back without missing a beat.

He was such an ass. Coy shouldn't give Law extra chances to insult him like this. "On that note, I guess I'll go spend a few hours on my appearance, since that's all I have to offer. Who knows? Maybe I'll snag a sugar daddy and I'll never have to work another day."

Law leaned against the stall door beside him, settling in as if he could trade insults all day. "I thought that's what you've been doing since David took you in."

That one stung. Coy took it in the chest. If anyone knew how Coy would never feel like he'd repay David for taking him in, it was Law. It seemed Coy was right to feel like he'd never be good enough to deserve to be rescued. Coy couldn't even dredge up a response. No matter what mask he wore, inside, Coy always looked exactly the way he had the day David brought him home—covered in deep cuts and bruises. Without thought, Coy shook his head. King's voice was still in there, telling him that he deserved nothing. Coy turned and walked away, hoping to leave the phantom pains behind. King was dead. He tried remembering the tricks his counselor had taught him to shake these moments. Nothing penetrated the instant darkness inside him, except one thought. It was funny how Law was the only person who ever triggered him. How sick was Coy that he couldn't stop begging for it?

COY WOULDN'T BE ALONE. Law couldn't take it. His throat burned. Even he recognized how hypocritical he was for being angry. The knowledge doubled when his phone dinged with an incoming message. He knew immediately who it would be.

Law didn't bother looking until he was closed inside his bedroom, where no one could see how unexcited he was by hearing from Tracy.

Tracy: *Can't wait to see you. I'm home from work, so I'll be ready on time.*

Law: *Yeah, I'm done for the day too. I'll be on time.*

With a growl, Law tossed the phone onto the bed and scrubbed his hands over his face. Fuck. His. Life. Coy's face when he'd walked away. Law's chest hurt. He'd gone too far. Law didn't know how to stop. He was just so goddamn angry at the idea Coy wouldn't be alone tonight. As far as he knew, this was the first time that had happened since Coy came to live with them. At just the thought of that day, an ache bloomed in Law's chest. Coy looked just like an angel. Blond hair. Blue eyes. Dimples. That day, though, all Law had seen were the cuts and bruises. Full handprint bruises had covered Coy's arms. His face had been a mess of dark contusions. His sexy blue eyes had been flat and dead. Law's throat swelled. The rage he'd experienced at the first sight of Coy hadn't lessened. It didn't matter the man responsible had killed himself months ago. Law wanted to dig him up and kill him again.

Despite the obvious abuse, it hadn't doused Coy's flame. A smile tugged at Law's lips. He hated confrontations with Coy, but Law couldn't stop pushing him. When Coy was angry, Law caught glimpses of Coy's soul. The boy was passion and fire, but he kept it buried—like he scared himself. There'd only been a handful of times Law had seen Coy's heart. One stood out from the others.

Coy's bare torso called to Law like a beacon. He was such a small guy Law hadn't realized how perfect Coy's body was. He was compact yet well-defined— like a dancer. Law imagined putting Coy in his pocket. His feet kept moving in Coy's direction. Coy glanced over his shoulder. He made no move to cover himself.

"I'm off the clock."

Law dipped his chin. "I know."

Coy's guilty expression didn't waver. It was obvious he expected Law to find a fault in him. "David said he didn't care if I used the pool."

A smile curved Law's lips. "This is your home."

Without thought, Law's hand lifted. His fingertips skimmed a long, deep scar down Coy's chest. Chill bumps rose on Coy's skin. Law ignored the hunger in his gut. "What happened here?"

Coy turned his head. He wasn't quick enough. Law saw the pain he tried to hide. Even though Law had known David had rescued Coy from an abusive relationship, every day something else would happen, forcing Law to understand Coy's life had been much worse than anyone suspected. Law wanted to make him better. He wanted Coy to heal. Pity wasn't the answer.

Law took a breath and pulled his shirt up before tossing it aside. He twisted at the waist and turned his badly scarred shoulder Coy's way. "I got this one at ten. The woman who gave birth to me was ironing her work clothes. She walked away to answer the phone, and I accidentally bumped the ironing board. The iron tipped over. While no one was watching, it burned her nurse's uniform. Right away, I knew I'd fucked up." He loathed talking about his past, but Coy needed to see Law's soul. "I swear I saw the devil in her. She screamed, raged, and broke shit. Finally, she snatched up the iron and said she'd show me what it was like to have something irreplaceable ruined." Law shrugged. "I think I blacked out for part of it."

Coy's palm came to rest on the scar. His fingertips lightly traced the lines. "She didn't show you anything."

Law's eyebrows rose in question.

Coy dropped his hand and looked away. He spoke while staring at the water. The blue tint of the pool made Coy's eyes even bluer. "You said she screamed she'd show you what it was like to have something irreplaceable ruined. You're still beautiful. She didn't show you anything."

Law's throat swelled at the memory. Before that moment, he hadn't known the exact words he needed to hear to steal the power from that horrible memory. Coy had given them to him. Law's body burned for Coy. He tugged at his clothes, stripping. Law fired his shower to life and stepped beneath the steady stream while the water was still ice cold. Coy wouldn't be alone tonight. Law pressed his forehead to the cool shower wall. With his eyes squeezed shut and where no one could see him, Law could be honest with himself. This was the only place he was allowed to be truthful. He didn't want to go out tonight. There was only one person he wanted, and they were already under this roof. All he had to do was go down the hall. Except there was nothing simple about wanting Coy. Law had dozens of reasons to stay away.

An image of Coy formed in his head. Law could picture Coy so clearly, it was as if he was there. He spent so much time staring at Coy that he could imagine even the tiniest of details. His wicked smile. The way he scrunched up his forehead when concentrating. Law's hand slid down his stomach. Coy's eyes were amazing. They constantly changed with his mood. When he was happy, they were brighter than usual. They flashed with anger more often than not, but—sometimes—he'd look Law's way and his eyes would darken. Law's hand dipped lower, colliding with his cock. A shot of lust hit Law in the gut. He hissed as he massaged his aching dick. Law hated himself a little. Self-hatred was a familiar state for Law. Coy deserved better than to have Law jacking off to his image. Law couldn't stop.

At forty-three, if Law hadn't met anyone who could win him, then chances were good he never would. Coy was different. He was off-limits for more reasons than Law could count. Law burned for him. A tiny part of Law hated Coy for it. This boy, what did he have no one else did? Fuck, Law could see him on his knees. He could practically feel Coy's hot mouth. Law stroked his cock, picturing Coy looking up at him while his tongue toyed with Law's crown. Law pumped faster. Would Coy accept his cum or wipe it away? Would he let Law kiss him afterward?

His balls drew up tight. Law ground his back teeth. Every muscle in his body tensed. The image in his head changed. Coy's lips brushed his. Law's throat swelled. Coy pressed his mouth to Law's ear and whispered his love. Law exploded. A gasp reverberated off the walls of the shower as an orgasm rocked him. Law couldn't breathe. No one could know. He could never let anyone find out. It was too late for him. Coy had stolen his heart months ago. No one could ever know.

THREE

It turned out, when life went to shit, Jonah was always the person to call. Not only had Coy not thought about Law once all night, he couldn't breathe from laughing. Jonah knew everyone. He'd called a friend who had a friend, and Coy found himself inside a posh, exclusive nightclub he hadn't known existed. A party of Jonah's friends had been waiting inside.

So far, his favorite was Wyld West. It seemed he owned the club where they were currently dancing. He'd shown up, sexy husband in tow, no shirt, and ready to party. Every time Jonah tried to make a break for it to get a drink, one of Jonah's many friends hauled him back into the throng of bodies gyrating on the dance floor. There was no rhythm to anyone's steps. No fucks were given. They were all sober and the craziest people he'd ever met. They were fresh air right when he'd been drowning.

Coy snagged Jonah's waist and badly kept time with his bouncing in place to press his lips to Jonah's ear. "Thank you for this." He was forced to yell the words to be heard.

"Of course," Jonah yelled back. "We're friends. I want you to smile."

Because Jonah demanded it, Coy smiled as bright as he could. Before he could say anything else, some guy crashed into him. Coy swallowed a shot of unexpected fear. He turned and came face to face with the guy's wicked smile. "Sorry," the guy yelled before moving on. No harm done. Coy's heart slid back into place, no longer choking him. A slow song started. Bodies paired, and couples flooded the dance floor. Coy held his side and headed toward the bar. He needed a drink. His throat burned from dehydration and laughing. Before Coy made it ten steps, a hand slid across the small of his back. A strong arm encircled his waist. Coy turned. His chest collided with Law's. Their bodies molded. Coy's feet automatically kept pace with the music, even as his mind remained frozen. He didn't know where Law had come from. It was as if Coy's heart had conjured him from thin air. He couldn't look away from Law's gorgeous face. His jaw was even harder than usual—like Coy had somehow managed to piss him off more than normal.

Coy's mind thawed. His hands saw their chance and slid up Law's solid chest. Damn. Law's body was even harder than Coy expected. It was as if Law's every muscle was tensed to pounce or flee. Coy's hands kept going until they met behind Law's neck. Law's arms tightened around Coy's waist. His hand found its way beneath Coy's shirt. He caressed the small of Coy's back, skin on skin. Coy sucked in a sharp breath at the contact. The air felt ragged as it left his lungs. He burned. From head to toe, every inch of Coy craved Law. He never wanted the dance to end. Law felt too good pressed against him. He stared at Coy like he felt the same. Coy could barely breathe around the lust. They would be amazing when they came together. Coy felt it in his bones.

They would scratch and bite. Coy took another labored breath. He swore he could already hear Law's deep rumbling moans.

The slow beat in the air died, replaced by a faster one. Law dipped his chin, closing the distance between them. Hope filled Coy's chest so full, he expected to explode. At the last second, Law changed directions. His lips touched the shell of Coy's ear. "You're welcome. I just saved you from an old perv who had his sights set on you." Law released him and turned away, disappearing into the crowd. Coy's feet wouldn't budge. He stared at the gyrating bodies that had swallowed Law, taking him away. Hands tugged on Coy, pulling him into the same circle of wild dancing he'd been enjoying all night before Law appeared and crushed him.

"I need a drink." Coy didn't know if anyone heard. He also didn't care. Nothing mattered but the black hole currently swallowing him. He blindly stumbled toward the bar, pushing his way through the crowd. Nothing mattered except finding a way to oblivion. He hadn't felt this way in months. Not since a few weeks after they found his ex, King, dead. In one moment, Law had sucked the life and happiness from him. The hollow self-destruction that always lived inside his brain woke from its dormant state. No one cared about him, especially him. Maybe if he drank enough, he'd do the world a favor and die too. There was only one way to find out.

LAW'S BODY was on fire. Unfortunately, he didn't burn for the person he should. The one he was there with. Fuck. Why did it always have to be Coy? From the moment he'd arrived and spotted Coy on the dance floor, smiling and acting his age for once, Law hadn't looked away. Then life chose to test him. Tracy had gone to the restroom. The instant she'd disappeared, the music slowed. Coy headed in the opposite direction. Law's feet had moved without his permission. Without a single thought or care for anyone else, Law's hands had collided with Coy's body. There was no power in heaven or on earth that could've stopped him from pulling Coy into his arms at that moment. He'd savored every second, already planning how their night would end. Until the slow song ended, and he'd spotted Tracy watching them at the edge of the floor.

Her expression said everything it should. She couldn't trust Law long enough for a bathroom break. She didn't speak when Law reached her side. Instead, Tracy crossed her arms over her stomach and stared at nothing—like she was holding herself together or the anger in. Law didn't blame her. He didn't know how he'd looked while dancing with Coy, but he knew how he'd felt. If the whole world hadn't seen his heart, then the whole world was blind. Tracy wasn't stupid. That knowledge didn't stop Law from trying to dig his way out.

Law motioned toward the floor. "That was one of my employees." Nothing. Silence. "He looked like he needed rescuing."

"Let me guess. That's Coy."

Law's head whipped around. He focused on Tracy in surprise. Even Tracy's soft brown hair screamed with outrage, and then her light green eyes moved his way. Law almost took a step back, but he never backed down from anything. "That was a hell of a lucky guess," Law said, keeping his voice as steady as he could beneath her knowing stare.

"Not really. You said his name no less than four times at dinner. I think I'll get a cab." Without another word, Tracy dipped between tightly pressed bodies and headed for the door. With a growl, Law went after her. Five steps into his chase, Law's feet planted. His body refused to budge. There was nothing he could say if he caught Tracy. The kindest thing he could do was let her leave. Halfway through dinner, Tyrone had texted him that David and he were headed to Wyld Nights—a well-known posh nightclub—and Law had been added to the VIP list if he'd like to join the party. Everyone was going, including Coy. The moment Ty mentioned Coy's name, Law had been incapable of refusing. His only hope had been Tracy's disinterest. Unfortunately, she'd been thrilled to receive an invite to one of California's most exclusive hot spots. Law had definitely ensured she'd gotten a night she wouldn't soon forget. It was better things ended this way. There had never been any chance of a happy ending.

Law caught sight of Coy at the bar. All thoughts of Tracy and his guilt disappeared. His heartbeat pounded in his ears. Coy tossed back shots like he could hoard them for later like a camel. A guy close to Law's age hovered nearby smiling and obviously cheering Coy on. Coy threw his head back, laughing at something the guy said, and then tried turning away. The guy snagged his arm. Law moved to intervene, seeing red. Before he reached them, the guy released Coy and ordered him more shots. Coy wasn't a big guy. Combine that with the fact that Coy hadn't drunk a drop of liquor as far as Law had seen since coming to live with David, Coy already looked unsteady. At the first sway, Coy's new friend sidled closer. His lips touched Coy's ear. Something inside Law snapped. He crossed the room and stepped between them, daring the dude with his eyes to say something.

"Time to go, Coy."

Coy smiled, visibly drunk. "I'm still having fun. Besides, John drove. I'm cool. Go back to whatever you were doing." He tried pushing his way past Law to get to his new friend. That wasn't happening.

Law threw out his hand, stopping him. "How about this? Drink as much as you want as long as you don't die. I'll pay and drive you home, as long as you stick to my side and let me make sure you're safe."

Coy tapped his chin, smiling as he pretended to think things over. "You are very big and good at watching over me."

Despite the situation, Law found himself smiling, the guy at his back forgotten. No one else existed but Coy. "It's a talent."

Coy cut his eyes at him in an adorably sexy way. "I thought you had a date tonight."

Law rubbed the back of his neck. A smile pulled at his lips. "Oh, you know, I combined my senior citizen discount with the early bird special and called it a night. You know how us old people are." Without thought, he swiped his fingers through Coy's sexy blond hair. It was a mess, and still he was hotter than anyone else there. "I see you spent hours on your appearance. Sexy, as always. If you haven't snagged a sugar daddy yet, maybe you could spare a dance for me."

Coy's light blue eyes flashed with humor. "Do you mean one where you're not rescuing me?"

"Yep. Just for the fun of it."

"I mean, you are taking me home," Coy said, toying with the buttons on Law's shirt. "It only seems fair." That was all the warning Law got before Coy dragged him onto the dance floor. Coy tossed back shots between songs and forced Law to dance to shit he never would have otherwise. As he'd always suspected he would, Law had a better time with Coy than he had in years. Law still kept a close watch on Coy's alcohol intake. At the first slurred word, Law found John and let him know he would see Coy home. Getting Coy in the truck when he wasn't ready to leave was an adventure in itself. Coy tried several times to head back inside. He didn't give up until Law pinned him against his chest. Then Coy melted into his hold, forcing Law to grind his back teeth to fight back the waves of lust. Goddamn, Coy smelled amazing. He made Law's mouth water. There was nothing appealing about a drunk. It was like Coy was incapable of turning Law off. As Law lifted Coy into the truck and buckled his seatbelt, he stole more touches than necessary.

"You're being so nice tonight," Coy muttered, sounding out of his head. "Why do you only like me when no one is watching?"

Coy's question stole Law's breath. He deserved the jibe and so much worse. It wasn't like he didn't know he always hurt Coy. But Coy didn't understand. Law couldn't be what Coy wanted. "I always like you. You shouldn't like me," Law said, hoping Coy didn't hear. He closed the door before Coy responded. Law took his time circling the truck. His temper irrationally spiked. Lately, his moods were all over the place and hard for him to control. As he slid behind the wheel, the ugliness pressing on his brain disappeared. Coy had his head leaned back on the seat, already half asleep. He was adorable.

"Coy?" He didn't respond. Law swiped his fingers through Coy's hair. Coy still didn't budge. "I think you're perfect."

Coy's head shot up. He blinked at his surroundings. "Did you say something?"

"Yeah. You should rest your eyes."

Coy nodded and relaxed again. Law drove home in silence. His gaze kept sliding Coy's way. The temptation to reach over and touch Coy was massive. Law couldn't think about anything else. Soon they'd be home and Law would go to bed alone. Tomorrow, things would return to normal. Law already missed Coy's smile.

Inside the garage, Law pulled his keys from the ignition but didn't get out. For a moment, he simply stared at Coy. He looked uncomfortable. Law shook his head. It was over. He needed to let Coy sleep.

Sitting there all night would change nothing. Law silently slipped from the truck and moved to Coy's side. Coy came awake the second Law touched him. Law fought the urge to hold Coy to his chest and carry him in the house.

Instead, he became the man Coy hated. "Come on, drunkard. Once again, you're leaving all the heavy lifting to me." In one smooth motion, he tossed Coy over his shoulder.

"Jesus," Coy breathed.

"Don't you dare puke on me."

"I'm good."

Law snorted but didn't call bullshit.

"You have such a nice ass," Coy said, stroking Law's ass. Law bit his bottom lip to keep from laughing. From Coy's position on Law's shoulder, he should've had a hard time talking. Nothing slowed Coy while inebriated, it seemed. "You're so pretty. Why do you have to be so pretty?" Coy stroked his ass again, even as his voice turned sad. "Maybe if you were ugly, I wouldn't be so stupid when it comes to you. I doubt it, but maybe."

Law shook his head at Coy's antics. "You're probably going to hate yourself tomorrow if you don't stop talking."

"Probably," Coy said, sounding ridiculously level headed. "Since I always hate myself, tomorrow will be just another day. As a matter of fact, you usually hate me too. We have so much in common. You have a great ass. I'm gonna touch it." He was true to his word. Coy squeezed his butt. "Law?"

Coy's three-sixty spin to a sad tone hurt Law's throat. "Yeah?"

"If I could be different to make someone else happy, it would be you."

Law's eyes fell closed. He took a deep breath for strength. Unfortunately, Coy's cologne filled his nose instead. "I don't want you to be different." Law pushed the back door open as he made the claim. Coy didn't say anything while Law made his way through two hallways, avoiding any chance of encountering anyone on the way to Coy's bedroom. He stopped a few feet from Coy's door.

"You should take me to bed."

Law bent at the knees to set Coy on his feet. "You've had a lot to drink. You should go to bed alone before you make a fool of yourself." In his head, the words sounded scathing. Leaving his lips, Law's words sounded breathless as Coy's body slid down his as Law set Coy on his feet. His arms didn't release Coy the way Law's brain demanded. Coy touched Law's chest. Their feet shuffled closer. Law dropped his chin. He couldn't look away from the way Coy fingered the top button on Law's shirt. Their temples met. Neither of them moved away.

With their heads together and their faces only inches apart, Law's breathing shallowed. He was half terrified and fully aroused. Coy slipped the buttons loose on Law's shirt. All Law could do was watch it happen. His body refused to budge. His fingers wouldn't unclench from where they held Coy's waist. Law's shirt fell open. He could feel Coy breathing every bit as heavily. He turned his head. Their lips bumped. It wasn't a kiss, but Law automatically leaned his head away. If they kissed, Law was lost. He didn't think he could turn back from tasting Coy. Coy didn't chase him. Instead, he brushed his palm across Law's bare stomach. Law dropped his chin again. This time, when Coy's lips

29

brushed his, Law held still. His breathing was so shallow, he wondered if he'd faint. Coy made no attempt to deepen the kiss.

Coy leaned away an inch. "You're right," he whispered, sounding broken. "I've had a lot to drink. I should go to bed before I make a fool of myself." Coy tried turning away.

Law's hold tightened on Coy. Coy didn't lift his chin or meet his stare. Law could practically feel the hurt rolling off Coy. The way Law pulled and pushed Coy all the time, fighting himself, was hurting Coy. That was not what Law wanted. He didn't know how to stop. "I should've let you go home with Jonah."

Coy's sexy light blue gaze finally lifted at the claim. Law swore he saw something harden and die. He couldn't breathe at the idea. "I think I'm done letting you stand on me so you can feel taller. Maybe I am a fool, sad, and stupid like everyone tells me, but at least I'm not a coward. If you ever decide to be honest with yourself, I don't think you can say the same."

Law's arms fell away. He watched in silence as Coy disappeared inside his bedroom. For longer than he cared to admit, Law stared at Coy's closed door. Coy's accusations rang in Law's ears. He didn't need to search his heart. Law had known he was a coward for years. Until tonight, he hadn't realized he was also a bad person.

FOUR

Not once had Coy crossed Law's path since the incident after the club. Coy had always been good at avoiding him, but this was nuts. After spending two entire nights tossing and turning, Law had decided he would apologize. If nothing else, he owed it to Coy to say he was sorry and leave him alone. He'd known all along they wouldn't be together. It was possible Coy's claim was true. Maybe Law had been standing on him to feel taller, in a sense. He would stop. Somehow. Even if it killed him. Damn. Law rubbed his chest. He was pretty sure it would kill him.

After ten minutes of hunting on his own, Law gave up and searched out Rick. The older, rugged-looking cowboy sat on an overturned bucket and watched as the other guys acclimated themselves to the two new horses David had bought.

"Where's Coy?"

Rick shrugged. He didn't look Law's way. "I haven't seen him today. I assumed you'd sent him to do something else."

With a growl, Law headed for the house. If David hadn't sent Coy on errands without telling Law, Law would put his foot in Coy's ass. It was one thing for Coy to be pissed off at Law. It was a whole other thing for him to leave the crew shorthanded like a petulant child. He found David in his office. Law tried bringing his rage under control as he tapped his knuckles on David's open door.

David glanced up. "Hey, Law. What's up?"

Law held his straw cowboy hat between his hands as he crossed the threshold. "Have you seen Coy? It seems he left the crew shorthanded today."

"They're not shorthanded," David said, going back to shuffling through the paperwork on his desk. "We're in our slow season."

David's cold tone gave Law pause. He also didn't fail to notice David hadn't answered his question. "And Coy?"

"He left."

"Okay," Law said, dragging out the word.

With a loud sigh, David met his stare again. His light blue eyes weren't exactly hard, but they weren't as welcoming as usual. "Coy gave me his notice yesterday. He asked to work out his two weeks with Tyrone instead of here. After hearing his reasons, I chose to let him go ahead and leave. No hard feelings or bad references."

Law spent a moment debating whether he should ask or run.

Before he decided, David's expression softened, and he motioned Law closer. "Close the door and have a seat."

Shit. He should have run while he had the chance. Law closed the door and then chose the chair across from David.

"Would you like to tell me your side of things?"

At David's question, Law forced his hands to still before he twirled his cowboy hat again. "Not really, no."

David's expression never wavered. He didn't look disappointed or angry, merely resigned. "Either way, I intend to speak my piece." Law wouldn't have expected anything less. David wasn't the type to stay silent in a time like this. He was beyond generous and a good man, but he wouldn't hold his tongue while Law seduced a much younger employee in his care. "You've always been harder on Coy than anyone else. At first, I thought you didn't want him to think you pitied him after the way he came to us. But months passed, and you didn't let up." It was true. All of it. Law couldn't deny it. Still, getting called on his actions made him feel like shit. "I've asked myself why many times, but never quite came up with a theory that felt right. Coy is a hard worker. He's always gone above and beyond. As far as I could tell, he's never deserved the unfair treatment. But still, I told myself you must have reasons I hadn't seen. Now, though, it's cost us a good employee, so I'm no longer stabbing at theories. I'm demanding an answer. Did Coy do something to deserve being made to feel unwelcome these past months?"

For a moment, Law was confused. Coy hadn't told David about the other night, or all the other near misses when Law had almost given in to temptation. Law stared at David without blinking. He couldn't think of a single plausible explanation that didn't make Coy or him look bad.

Another tired-sounding sigh escaped David. He scrubbed at his forehead. "Look, Law. We've known each other forever. You're family. There's really nothing you can say to me right now that would make me think badly of you, but I need you to say something. The truth, preferably."

Law lost the battle against his nervousness and twirled his hat between his hands. "It's all on me," he said finally. "Like you said, Coy always worked hard. I didn't ride his ass to keep him in check. I did it to keep me in check." David's expression didn't change. There wasn't an ounce of judgment on David's face, so Law kept talking. "I don't know what Coy said to you, but I swear I never meant to hurt him. I'll do whatever you want here. If you want me to talk to him and convince him to come back, I will. If you'd prefer I step away from my position, I will."

David pulled a face. "Don't be ridiculous. I couldn't run this place without you." David stacked some papers together. "And Coy didn't complain about you. Coy isn't the type to whine. It's my opinion you were too hard on him. In his shoes, I would've left a lot sooner. As far as convincing Coy to come back, you'd have to find him first. He was gone half an hour after I said he didn't have to work out his notice."

Law's brow furrowed. "Gone?"

"Yes, gone," David repeated. "He packed his clothes, called for a cab, and left."

Law stared at nothing, trying to come to terms with what he was hearing. "Wait. If Coy didn't give his notice because of me, why did he quit?"

"I didn't say it wasn't because of you," David said without missing a beat and cutting Law to the bone. "I said Coy didn't complain. Instead, he explained how he wasn't good at this job, no matter how hard he tried. He felt he was letting everyone down, no matter how I argued to the contrary. In the end, I decided it would be doing him more harm than good by forcing him to work out his notice. Nine months of beating down his self-esteem is enough, don't you think?"

Law wanted to argue it hadn't all been bad. Instead, all he could think about was Coy's well-being. "Where would he go? He doesn't have anywhere else to go." Law fought back the panic threatening to swallow him whole. David was one of the few people who understood why the idea of Coy running away to face homelessness would leave Law feeling like he was suffocating.

"I'll take over the crew for the rest of the day while you find him," David said, releasing Law from the hell forming in his mind. "Start with Jonah. He'd be my first guess. You won't have to go far either. Jonah volunteers at Tyrone's clinic on Mondays."

Law stood. "I don't know if it'll help, but I'll find him and apologize."

David leaned back in his chair, stretching, as if he'd been stooped over paperwork for hours. "Apologizing always helps, even if it doesn't fix anything." He focused on Law, looking lost. "Honestly, I have to admit I thought things would be different between you two. I thought, if anyone could understand, it would be you. I'd really hoped—maybe—you'd be the way Dad was with you."

Except Law didn't feel the least bit fatherly toward Coy. "Like I said, it's all on me. Maybe I see too much of myself in him." It was partially true. The rest of the truth was for him alone.

The way David watched him said he saw too much. Knew too much. "Maybe."

Law nodded and headed for the door before David said anything more. Even though David was the best person Law knew, this wasn't something they could talk about. If Law stayed, he might admit he was in love with Coy, and he didn't know how to stop. Nothing could ruin Coy's life faster.

WORKING for Tyrone was easy money as far as Coy was concerned. No one followed him around, critiquing his work or telling him to hurry. He simply moved from task to task in peace. Technically, he was volunteering today. His new job, cleaning the building, wouldn't start until late at night when there wasn't a full staff underfoot. Coy hadn't wanted to stay home alone in Jonah's ridiculously huge house all day, so he'd tagged along to volunteer with Jonah. Not only did it give him something to keep him out of trouble, it gave him a chance to get a head start on his cleaning. Sooner or later, he'd adjust to a new life. For now, nothing felt right. Things would get better once he was in his own place... he hoped.

Jonah had a house for rent and Coy had money saved. Working a good paying job with free room and board had made his bank account happy these past months. The cleaning position didn't pay as well since it wasn't as many hours. Eventually, that would be an issue. It was no big deal, though. Coy already had some feelers out for a full time day job. He didn't mind working two places. Working filled his hours and kept his mind busy. Since Coy had no interest in ever dating again, the busier he stayed the better. Just the thought of dating brought an image of Law to mind. Coy stared at the paper towel dispenser he'd been filling, seeing nothing. Law had probably shrugged and moved on with his day when he'd learned Coy was gone. Maybe. It was a pain for them to be shorthanded. An ache bloomed in his chest. He remembered the last time someone had walked off the job.

"What are you doing right now?"

Coy jumped and spun at the boomed question. Law looked more pissed than usual. Coy's mind scrambled, trying to decide if he'd done anything wrong. "Cleaning out the horses' stalls." Even Coy heard the question in his tone. He'd read today's schedule right, he thought.

Law motioned for Coy to follow. "Leave that for now. I'll help you finish it later. I need your help outside. Fucking Kerry quit without notice, leaving me short on help."

Coy picked up the pace to walk at Law's side. "Why did Kerry quit?"

"He wanted next week off, but Rick is already off next week. I told him if Rick would swap schedules with him, it was fine. Rick wouldn't swap, so Kerry left. I don't blame Rick. He's already paid for a trip out of town with his family. It's not easy to swap schedules on short notice."

It was nice to talk to Law when he wasn't the one in trouble. Coy kept up his side just to hear Law's deep voice. He liked the way it rumbled in his throat. "What did Kerry need to do on such short notice that it warranted quitting?"

Even Law's derisive snort was sexy. "All his boys were headed to Vegas. He was the only one who wouldn't get to go if he couldn't get off work. Good luck having money to blow in Vegas with no job. I don't re-hire people who fuck over the crew."

It was odd how much it bothered him that Law had been left in a bind. Law was always hard on him, but he was good to everyone else. Plus, Coy understood why Law gave him a hard time. Coy was a fuck-up. He rarely did anything right or made any good choices. He wanted to help. Coy took a breath, hoping he didn't regret his next words. "I don't have anything else going on. If you need some extra help, I don't mind working late to cover for Kerry and my duties until you can replace him."

"I know you don't mind, because you're an amazing person. That's exactly why I would never expect that of you."

Coy missed a step. Not only had Law actually complimented him, he hadn't paused to think—like it *was common knowledge and not just an opinion. Coy had no words. Occasionally, he saw flashes of a human inside Law. Those glimpses were what kept him fascinated. Sometimes, he thought if Law ever showed his true face, Coy might lose himself completely.*

"You're doing such a great job."

The brightly spoken words startled Coy enough he dropped half the paper towels he held. "Fuck. Sorry."

"Don't be sorry," Jonah fussed as he stooped to help Coy pick up his mess. "I'm the one who sneaked up on you." Jonah handed his stack to Coy once they'd managed to pile up the paper towels. "Hey, I wanted to tell you that it looks like you'll have the place to yourself tonight. John just texted me to be ready to go out of town for the night. Now's your chance to throw a kegger."

Coy could tell by Jonah's smile he was joking, but Jonah had been too good to him. Coy couldn't stop his internal freak out from leaking from his mouth. "I would never do that you after all you've done."

Jonah's smile fell. A hint of concern flashed in his sweet brown eyes. "Oh, honey, I know. It was a joke. You're not the type to take advantage of anyone." He rubbed Coy's arm as he made the claim. Coy's heartbeat slowed. Jonah was such a cutie with his purple scrubs, messy brown hair, and gorgeous heart. Coy wished he'd met Jonah sooner, before life had kicked the shit out of Coy and left him bitter. Jonah's expression turned even more understanding, punching Coy in the throat. "I know you feel like an outsider at my place, but you shouldn't. Think of it as a vacation until John's lawyer gets the lease drawn up on my old house and the people fixing it up are finished."

Coy took a deep breath. Life fit him like skinny jeans. Somehow, he'd gotten into them, and now he wondered if he'd have to cut his way out if he hoped to ever breathe properly again. "I promise I'm trying."

A quiet knock cut Jonah off before he had to explain he wasn't good at functioning at an adult level. He turned toward the door. Law hovered in the doorway, looking ready to bolt.

Jonah was the first to react. "I have something else to do," he said, making a run for it. He didn't try hiding the obvious attempt to make himself scarce. Jonah leapt from the room like a fire blazed around them. Maybe the room was burning. Coy fully expected the ceiling to crash down on him at any moment. His gaze wouldn't budge from Law. He looked the way he always did. Old work boots, straw hat, and jeans that hugged every gorgeous line. Coy swallowed hard. He stared at the way Law's black t-shirt clung to his chest. He'd caressed that chest. At the thought, Coy's chin snapped up. He focused on Law's face. Law had rejected him. Left him feeling humiliated and undesirable. Coy was unwanted, but fuck Law. It wasn't all in Coy's head. Law knew what was what. He'd given Coy just enough to keep him hanging on. Strung him along. Coy wasn't crazy.

"You quit."

Coy blinked. Law's voice sounded different—like it hurt to speak. "Yeah."

"I needed you today."

Like an idiot, Coy's heart turned over at Law's claim. He hugged the paper towels to his chest, hoping to protect the foolish organ that clung to the hope Law might want him someday. "I'm sure you'll find a replacement in no time. Lots of people need work."

Law shook his head. "I need you."

Coy's stupid heart raced. Every second that passed in Law's company made it harder for Coy to breathe. "Why?" Fuck. He was like the village idiot or something. Anyone else would've told Law to go fuck himself. Not Coy. He was ready to do whatever Law asked because he was too dumb to save himself.

"David bought a new horse today. She's jumpy and a biter. You're amazing with horses and the two of you already have something in common. She hates me too."

A lump rose in Coy's throat. He swallowed hard. His brain screamed for him to deny it. Coy's lips wouldn't form that lie. There was a part of him that did hate Law, because he loved him, and Law would never feel the same. "You don't re-hire people who fuck over the crew."

"You didn't."

"Get Rick to care for her," Coy shot back. The anger he should've felt upon seeing Law finally reared its head.

"I need you."

Coy immediately deflated. Law was the only person he didn't know how to fight. He was one person one minute and someone else the next.

"Please?"

Turning his back on Law, Coy crammed the paper towels in the dispenser to give himself a moment. He couldn't let Law see how that one word gutted him. "I already have a new job, but it's at night." He kept his back turned. Coy didn't know if he could survive much longer under Law's stare. "If you need my help, I have a few hours free before I need to get to work." Coy's eyes fell closed as he made the offer. It was like ripping out his heart and handing it to Law. He didn't know how to stop setting his soul on fire to warm other people.

"I'll have you to your new job on time, and I'll make sure you're paid double time for helping us out today."

After locking the dispenser, Coy managed to face Law once more. "I'll let Jonah know I'm headed out." Law didn't show any disappointment or triumph. His face remained clear. That was the only thing saving Coy from coming apart at the seams. Now all he had to do was make it through the rest of the day. He could do that. Maybe. Hell, he was fucked.

WHILE LAW TRIED his damnedest to stay focused on the road, he could feel Coy's stare. Everything about this was a bad idea. He should've let Coy go. The idea of Coy hating him was too much. He had to try for some middle ground. Law cleared his throat. The silence in the truck was crushing his soul.

"So, you have a new job already."

It hadn't been a question. Thankfully, Coy took it as one and didn't force Law to dig. "Yeah. Before Ty was shot, he offered me a job cleaning his building at night. I decided I'd take it. It's not as much money as working for David. Plus, no room and board, but you know."

Yeah, Law knew. Coy wouldn't have Law destroying his life while working for Ty. In truth, he was a little surprised Coy willingly spoke about Ty getting shot, even if it was just in passing. Coy's ex had been the one to nearly kill Ty. It was an issue for him. Law tried staying on track. "Where will you stay?"

"With Jonah, for now. Don't worry over it. I'll figure it out. After all, I'm like a cat, right?"

Law tried for a smile that wouldn't come. "You always land on your feet."

"No," Coy said, sounding cold and absent. "I'm very adept at getting other people to take me home."

Ouch. Law deserved that dig. "That's because you're a good person." To his amazement, Coy fell silent once again. Normally, neither of them backed down from a sparring match. Law was exhausted from fighting Coy. He just wanted to be with him. Yet, by the time they made it to the stables, Law couldn't get away fast enough. Coy's anger and hurt was choking him. Law didn't know how to make it right. He drove past the sprawling brick home they'd shared only days ago. Law didn't look its way. He noticed Coy didn't either. At the stables, Law leapt from the truck like it was set to explode and headed inside. Coy followed at a slower pace.

When they reached the third stall inside the large barn, Law motioned toward the half door and the horse on the other side. "This is Belle."

"Awww," Coy said, immediately moving close and petting Belle with no fear. "She's so pretty. I love the spotted saddle horses." Without an ounce of hesitation, he popped the door's lock and slipped inside the stall with Belle. Unlike with Law, she stood still and seemed to relish his attention. Law moved closer. She immediately danced in place in protest.

Law backed up a step. "I'll let you get to know her, and I'll come back in a little bit. Maybe you can get her settled." He didn't wait for Coy to argue before walking away. Even to Law, his long stride felt angry as he made his way toward the house. He didn't bother driving. Law was too angry. He didn't know why he was so pissed. That wasn't true. Life was unfair. He'd stayed on the ranch, refusing David's father's offers of expensive schools and a life mimicking David's. Law had chosen a reclusive existence for a reason. He'd never imagined that life would find him where he stood still. That all the things he couldn't have would move into his home and become a constant dirt in his wounds. He never dreamed of Coy. Now he knew his loss. It left him bitter.

By the time Law made it to David's office, his temper was through the roof. This time, he didn't bother knocking. "He's here. I hope you're happy."

David's eyebrows rose at the impressive entry. "What?"

Law motioned helplessly in the direction of the stables. "Coy. He's here. We've talked. You can feel better about your brotherly duties."

David's eyebrows smoothed. "Oh. Is he working here again?"

It took all Law's control not to stamp his feet in his frustration. David had always been maddening. "That ship has sailed, but he's here. You got your wish."

"Law—"

"I really don't want to hear whatever you're about to say next, David."

"I'm not blind. Or stupid," David added, his voice heavy with understanding that Law couldn't handle at the moment.

Law took a deep breath. He didn't want to fight. They might not be related by blood, but David was his brother in all the ways it counted. Over the years, they'd fought like it many times, but not about this. This was his. "I love you, David, but for once, I need you to leave it alone."

"But he—"

"Leave it alone, David. I'm happy you're happy, having found your other half after all these years of working yourself into the ground, but I'm not you. Please? Stay out of it."

David gave a jerky nod. Law didn't feel better. He'd known he wouldn't. David was all the family he had. He was the only person who cared about Law. But loving Coy hurt and no one understood. Law had to do things his way because there was no other way. He had nothing to offer anyone, especially someone who deserved love—like Coy did.

COY SPENT the next hour waffling between obsessing over the way Law had bolted and telling himself he was done. Belle was sweet. It was possible Law would need to find someone else to care for her, but there was nothing wrong with her. Law was surly. She wouldn't do well with a cranky bastard caring for her. Coy got it. After all, he'd run away from this ranch for the same reason. Coy suppressed a snort. Maybe he should take up biting too. He smiled at the thought. It wouldn't win him any friends, but not chomping on people hadn't gained him anything either. It was a thought.

"How's it going?"

Coy glanced up from where he sat on an overturned bucket inside the stall. "Good. She's settled down a lot." As if intent on making a liar of him, Belle nipped at Law, barely missing him.

"Damn. She really doesn't like me. I've never encountered this with an animal before."

Coy stood and brushed off his ass. "I don't think it's you, per se." He held on to her mane and pointed at her back legs. "If you look back here, she has a lot of thin white scars. Someone beat her, probably trying to achieve a certain gait or whatever. Between that and your size, I imagine she's intimidated. It's not that I'm better. I'm just smaller. Let's try this." Coy moved to the door and opened it for Law. He kept one hand pressed to Belle's neck, stopping her from turning on Law and biting him as he passed. "Get in here."

Law moved slow, slipping behind Coy. Their bodies collided. Coy's eyes fell closed. He didn't know if the move had been intentional on Law's part, but damn. Law's body was solid and warm. Coy hated himself in that moment. No matter how hard he fought or far Law pushed him away, Coy couldn't stop feeling everything for Law.

With the door latched again, Coy stroked Belle's neck, staying near her head so she couldn't get to Law. She danced in place, making Coy wonder if she'd squish them both against the wall in her agitation. "Pet her," Coy said when Law didn't budge.

Law dutifully ran his palms down Belle's spine. After a few stamps and noises, she settled down. Side by side, they calmed Belle. Coy could feel the heat rolling off Law's skin from where he stood too close. Coy finally managed to take a step back. He moved at a crawl, in case he had to leap forward again to stop Belle from biting. When she didn't react, Coy took another step back. Once he was fairly confident she wouldn't take a chunk out of Law, he reclaimed the homemade stool. Law didn't stop stroking Belle and making soothing sounds.

"See?" Coy said, keeping his voice calm and steady. "Sometimes, you just have to prove you're not like everyone else." Even Coy wasn't one hundred percent sure he meant Belle anymore.

Law glanced over his shoulder like he questioned who the statement had been referring to also. "How did a city boy end up knowing so much about horses anyhow?"

A soft chuckle escaped Coy at the question. Changing the subject was fine by him. "Well, as you can imagine, I was a bit of a handful growing up." He could tell by the curve of Law's cheek that he was smiling. That smile kept him talking. "I was raised by a single mother. She's a nurse practitioner, so even though we were a single income family, she could still afford to give me whatever I wanted. But it's also one of those jobs where she worked a crazy schedule and I was always home alone. So, during the summers, she would send me to all these crazy day camps. I'm being completely serious when I say that I got sent to every sports camp imaginable. All of them. Think of a sport. She made me try it." Coy stared at nothing. Nostalgia washed over him. He'd hated camp, but things had been so simple then. His life hadn't been uncomplicated or easy since. "I even got stuck doing six weeks of jujitsu. Little did I know, learning how to take a hit has come in handy." Coy didn't look at Law as he spoke. It was easier to keep talking when he didn't think about who listened. Law was extremely adept at finding him lacking. Coy didn't have the strength for that today. "Finally, she signed me up to volunteer at this horse camp for the blind. Never in the history of ever had I expected to hate something more." Despite his best efforts, his gaze slid Law's way. A smile touched his lips. "From day one, I loved it. I'm used to not being good at anything, but to my surprise, I wasn't bad at dealing with animals. I kept going back." Coy spread his arms wide before dropping them. "So that's me. How did you end up here?"

Law kept his back turned, but Coy still saw the way he tensed at the question. Obviously, Belle felt the change as well. She turned restless again. Before Coy jumped to his feet, she settled down. Law cleared his throat. "You already know part of the story." He cleared his throat again, sounding uncomfortable as fuck. "After the woman who gave birth to me tried ironing my skin off, I waited until she left for work and I ran away. I made it pretty damn far too for a skinny, malnourished little kid. With nothing but the shorts I had on and a ratty pair of shoes, I stuck to the woods. I kept thinking I would get eaten by a wolf or something. Just when I thought they'd probably never find my body, I stumbled into a vineyard. Of course, I didn't know it was a vineyard. All I saw were grapes for miles. Wine grapes are a special breed. They're bitter as hell, but I was stuffing my face like I hadn't eaten in years. Really, in a way, I hadn't. That's where Mr. Baker found me. Not the current one, of course," Law clarified. "His father, Tim. He took one look at me, scooped me up, and carried me to the house. I imagine it wasn't hard for him to figure me out, even though I refused to tell him anything other than my first name. There wasn't a doubt in my mind if I got sent back to the woman who birthed me after running away, no one really would find my body." Coy's eyes burned. He understood, and that made it so much worse. It was one thing for Coy to suffer. He couldn't fathom anyone harming Law. The idea of anyone hurting Law made Coy want to cry and fight. But he held his tongue because he wanted to hear Law's story even more. After a moment, Law cleared his throat again. "Anyhow, I'm not sure if Tim just decided to keep me and dared anyone to fight him, or if he paid off the woman who birthed me. Either way, this became my home, and I never saw her again. At first, I was scared of everything." Law chuckled. It was a sexy sound that made Coy's heart skip a beat. "Tim would simply pluck me from the ground and dump me on the nearest horse. My choices were to ride or die. That's pretty much how he taught everything— riding, swimming, and drinking." Coy could hear the humor in Law's voice. He couldn't help but smile along. "I used to sit at his side all the time, learning everything he was willing to teach me." Law's voice turned sad again. "I loved him. He was the only real parent I ever had."

"Where was David during all this?"

Law glanced over his shoulder as if he'd forgotten Coy was there. "Right there with us. In all the ways it matters, we're family. I never wanted to do anything other than be the person Tim taught me to be. From the moment he found me stealing his fruit, this has been my little piece of heaven."

Law's story left Coy with so many questions, but when his mouth opened, a confession escaped instead. "I don't have a place in the world. Not really. In truth, I don't care at all what I'm doing. It's a little odd, actually. If someone gives me a job, I do it, not really feeling one way or the other about it. I don't feel strongly about much of anything."

"Much of anything isn't nothing. What do you feel strongly about?"

Coy didn't answer. He couldn't. Law turned and met his stare. Coy didn't look away. He wasn't sure he even blinked. Coy refused to say the words, but he had no doubt Law could see the truth in his eyes.

"You didn't deserve the way I treated you."

Coy blinked, more than a little surprised by Law's admission. Law didn't stop there.

"There was never a day you didn't work your ass off while you were here. You always did a great job. Maybe you don't feel like you have a place, but you do. If you ever decide to come back, I'll have a spot for you."

"Wow." Even to Coy's ears, he sounded dry. But really. "That was..." Coy fought to put his thoughts into words. "... the least personal apology I've ever received." He stood. There was no reason for him to stay. He was tired of lying to himself that Law cared. Coy was exhausted from always loving people who felt nothing when they looked at him. "I need to get to work soon. There's no sense in you getting back out. I'll call a cab."

A panicked look passed over Law's features, confusing Coy. "You don't need a cab. I mean, you helped me out a lot today. How about I go with you and help you clean? That's the least I can do."

The fuck you that flew to Coy's tongue wouldn't fall from his lips no matter how badly he meant the words. "No. You've done enough." Coy didn't know if the pain or the anger would kill him first. All he knew was one would choke him if he stayed.

Law stepped into his path, blocking the door before he made his escape. Coy looked in every direction but Law's, because if he met Law's gaze, he would die. "Look at me."

"I can't." Even to Coy's ears he sounded desperate and ready to break.

Law cupped his face, leaving Coy no other choice than to hold his stare. He looked sad. Coy's throat swelled. "Coy, I—"

"Hey, boss. I'm clocking out for the day," Rick said, appearing outside the stall door.

Law moved away so fast Coy's head spun. "That's cool. I don't need you for anything else tonight."

Law's obvious fear over getting caught touching Coy was the final straw. Coy sidestepped him and pulled open the door. Before he made his getaway, Law snagged his arm and hauled him back inside the stall. Coy's heart raced into his throat. A yelp he couldn't control escaped him in his fear. His first instinct was to fight. Save himself. All he could hear was his heart pounding. All he felt was Law's fingers biting into his arm. Before his fist connected with Law's skin, Coy found himself crushed against the wall. The rough wood tore at his back. It didn't matter. Nothing mattered as Law's mouth covered his. Coy's hands flattened against Law's chest as their tongues met. Law's heart raced beneath Coy's palms. He breathed so fast, Coy wondered if Law would hyperventilate. He'd never kissed anyone so obviously scared to be kissing him. Coy stroked

Law's chest, hoping to calm him. Law shuffled closer. Law's kiss was so soft, it bordered on respectful. Coy tried deepening their kiss.

Law jumped away. "Goddamn it!"

Coy shrank at Law's open rage. He almost bolted until he caught sight of the blood running down Law's arm. It dawned on him. Belle had bitten him. Coy covered his mouth, trying not to laugh. That shit hurt. He knew. He'd been there.

"Let me see." There might've been a hint of humor in his tone.

Law eyed the horse, looking ready to fight, as he turned and showed Coy his wound. It was a small cut, but it looked like Belle had pinched the shit out of Law's skin before breaking through. Not to mention, it definitely needed to be disinfected.

"Let's get this cleaned up." He stroked Law's back. "You did good, babe. She was testing you."

Law glanced over his shoulder. Heat blasted from his eyes, nearly melting Coy's skin. "No. She was protecting you."

Coy swallowed. Belle might've been right in that. Coy didn't feel the least bit safe, and it was exhilarating. He'd never wanted anyone to destroy him as badly. Coy was certain it was only a matter of time before Law made him every bit as sorry as his expression promised. That was fine. Coy was up for the challenge. After all, it wouldn't be the first time he'd ended up completely destroyed.

FIVE

TWICE SINCE MOVING IN WITH JONAH, COY HAD
gotten lost on the trip to and from his bedroom on
the third floor. It was a house. How in the hell
someone got lost *in a house* was beyond him, but the
place was massive. David's home was too, but there,
he'd always kept to one side of the place, entering
through the back and sticking close to his bedroom.
Here, he felt freer to roam. He was slowly learning
his way around, but he wasn't always confident in
the direction he walked.

Coy checked his phone as he descended the steps.
He kept hoping to see Law's name waiting with a
message or a missed call. There was nothing. Not
even his mom had called in the past four days.

"There he is."

Coy's head snapped up at John's bellow. Jonah and John sat at the kitchen table with a third man Coy hadn't met. He was dark-haired and had green eyes that were almost unnaturally light. His suit looked as if it cost a fortune. Snazzy. He came to his feet as Coy moved farther into the room.

"This is our attorney, Brad Hollister," John said, motioning the man's way. "Brad, this is our houseguest, Coy."

Brad swiped his tie back inside his dark jacket as he stood and circled the table to shake Coy's hand. "Coy. Yes. Jonah has told me all about you. I understand you're interested in renting Jonah's old house."

Coy accepted his handshake. "Eventually. Hopefully. My last job, at Baker Ranch, provided room and board. Now I'm... homeless, I suppose," he said, feeling oddly nervous and reluctant to admit his current circumstances. Brad looked very put together. Coy felt like twice as big of a mess in Brad's presence.

Brad lifted one shoulder in a half shrug. "I recently went through a homeless stint myself. It happens."

"You?" Coy hadn't meant to say it, especially in such a disbelieving tone.

Brad laughed.

Coy snapped his mouth closed before his jaw dropped. Goddamn. The pretty boy lawyer was hot. Coy didn't usually go for the pretty ones. He liked bikers, tattoos, and cowboys with too much confidence. All the types that ultimately destroyed him. Coy couldn't think of a damn thing to say—like apologizing for his earlier disbelief. Thankfully, Jonah came to the rescue.

"John and I have to go to Viv's today. We were hoping you wouldn't mind accompanying Brad to check on the house. That way, you can look around and Brad can check on the progress of the crew that's been painting and whatnot."

Coy had a terrible feeling he was being set up, but it was Jonah. Coy couldn't say no. He pasted on a bright smile. "Sure. If Brad doesn't mind me hanging around, I don't have anything else to do today." Coy glanced Brad's way and caught the handsome lawyer checking him out. Brad smirked, unashamed at getting busted. Coy's mind skipped like a scratched record, making him forget his place in the conversation. He wasn't imagining things. Brad had definitely been looking him over like he was buying a new car. Damn. It had been too long since anyone showed any interest in him and wasn't ashamed. He'd forgotten how nice it was to be wanted, especially by someone as gorgeous as Brad.

"I'd love your company. We should get to know each other. Don't you think?"

Coy suppressed a shiver at Brad's blatantly sexual tone. He'd gotten out of the habit of flirting. Before Coy could think of an appropriate response, Jonah jumped in—all smiles. "Yes. This is an awesome idea." He pushed away from the table. "John and I have to go." The longing glance John cast toward his unfinished breakfast screamed they didn't have to leave quite yet, but it was Jonah. John would do whatever it took to make him happy.

Coy snatched up John's plate without thought. "Take your food with you." He might not get any say in Jonah's maneuvering, but he'd be damned if he pretended he didn't see Jonah's meddling for what it was.

Obviously not one to be one-upped, Jonah flashed him a smile. "He won't be needing that where we're going." At the open sex dripping from Jonah's tone, John blindly handed back the plate and jogged to keep up with Jonah.

As one, Brad and Coy cast each other knowing smiles. Like that, all discomfort fell away.

Coy shook his head. "They should be ashamed."

"Agreed," Brad said, taking the plate from Coy and setting it on the table. "On that note, I have no desire to stay here, being envious. Would you like to grab some breakfast before I show you the house?"

There was a nervous flutter in Coy's stomach, but he was suddenly ravenous. "I'd love to."

Brad's smile was sweet and welcoming. For once, Coy didn't think of Law at all. "After you," Brad said, motioning toward the door. He set his palm on the small of Coy's back as he reached past him and opened the door before Coy's hand touched the knob. Their gazes met and held. Coy's breath caught. Knowledge took hold. He would survive. Life had been nothing but shit for way too long, but Coy wasn't giving up. There was still hope, even if he never spoke to Law again. Coy would keep going. Surely he could endure one more heartbreak. Just one more.

SINCE COY MOVED OUT, Law hadn't slept easy. He'd never been good at sleeping. His nights always went one of three ways: he spent hours trying to fall asleep before finally crashing an hour before the alarm, he went to sleep right away, only to wake up wide awake several hours before the alarm, or he didn't sleep at all. It was a pattern he hadn't thought could get worse. Then Coy left. Now Law spent his nights waffling between berating himself for not sleeping and trying to decide if he should text Coy. Middle of the night texts were always bad. That was why Law had his phone resting face down on his chest while he stared at the ceiling.

When it came to Coy, Law had a million secrets. Some were his. Others were Coy's. One they shared —nightmares. He didn't know why Coy came to him that first time. Considering he'd never tried to endear himself to Coy, it made no sense for Coy to comfort him. Law thought about that night all the time.

A cold sweat coated Law's skin. Rapid breaths filled the air. His lungs burned, and his heartbeat pounded in his ears. A light tapping finally caught his attention. Law rushed across the room and tore open the door. Coy stood on the other side, wearing nothing except workout shorts. He rubbed his arm and shifted from foot to foot. It couldn't have been more obvious he didn't expect a warm welcome.

"Are you okay?"

Law nodded, feeling a bit stupid. "I had a bad dream. Sorry if I woke you." He couldn't even remember now what the dream had been about, but the horrible feeling something terrible happened still lingered. Law scrubbed his hand over his face and glanced down the hall. Coy's bedroom door stood open, but it was too far away for Coy to have heard him.

As if Coy read his mind, he shifted nervously again. "Sometimes I pace the hall. Nightmares," he added with a humorless smile.

Law stepped back and waved Coy inside. "Maybe if we keep each other company, we'll get tired again eventually."

Coy eased into the room, looking unsure of Law's plan. "I'm already so tired I can't think, but I still can't sleep."

He was so... sweet. Law wished ugliness had never brushed Coy's life. He might be jaded, but Law wasn't heartless. Law wanted Coy to have such a beautiful life he forgot ugliness existed. Law headed for the bed. "How about this?" He straightened the covers and then turned them down. "You get some sleep and I'll watch over you."

Coy's gaze moved from the bed to Law. "What about you?"

The black smudges beneath Coy's eyes said he needed the rest more than Law. "I'm good. Maybe next time, you can watch over me." He only added that last part to get Coy to agree. Law didn't need anyone.

"How about this instead?" Coy crawled onto the bed, settling on the opposite side. He grabbed a few pillows and made a line down the mattress. "Now you can join me without fear I'll molest you."

A bark of laughter escaped Law without warning. "First off, I'm not worried you'll molest me. Secondly, if you were set on taking advantage of me, I don't think pillows would stop anything." Even as he argued, Law climbed into bed with Coy. As ridiculous as the situation was, Law was oddly happy. Law played a lot of roles around Baker Ranch. None of them were intimate. In fact, it was important he stay detached from everyone. Law liked it that way. Coy made it impossible not to care.

As Coy settled into his spot, Law tucked him in. Even he didn't know why he couldn't stop fussing over Coy. Maybe it made him feel better about his weaknesses. Coy looked even younger, unguarded with nothing but the soft light of a tiny lamp in the corner.

"Is it okay if we leave that light on?"

Law curled onto his side, facing Coy. "I never turn it off," he admitted. After years of never knowing if he'd find himself attacked in the middle of the night, Law couldn't sleep in the dark. At some point, it became habit. They had a lot in common. Maybe all their common ground was bad, but Law knew they wouldn't judge each other.

Coy's eyes fell closed. His breathing deepened. Law didn't look away. The constant flutter in his chest worried him a bit. Still, his eyes never budged.

"Law?"

Law's breath caught at Coy's sweet tone. His eyes didn't open, and Law didn't know if Coy was awake or searching for him in his sleep. The thought alone punched him in the chest.

"Yeah?" he whispered, hoping not to wake him.

"It's okay if you go back to hating me in the morning. I understand."

A lump rose in Law's throat, choking him. It hurt his heart, knowing how easily Coy believed he wasn't worthy of anything. Not even someone's friendship. "I don't hate you." The words came too late. Coy's features had softened into sleep.

The phone buzzed on Law's chest, pulling him from his memories. His heart raced as he scrambled to open his messages.

Coy: *I had a nightmare.*

Law: *Can I come to you?*

Coy: *I'm already in a cab.*

Law: *You know where to find me.*

Right where he'd always be, waiting on Coy to need him. The twenty minutes it took for Coy to arrive felt more like hours. The moment the door quietly opened, Law rolled onto his side and lifted the covers, inviting Coy to join him. Coy dumped his phone and keys on the dresser, toed off his shoes, and tossed off his shirt before climbing under the covers. As one, they scooted closer until Law cradled Coy's back against his chest. Without thought, he dropped his mouth to Coy's shoulder and pressed a kiss to his skin. He froze as he realized what he'd done, but he didn't move away. His fingers found Coy's hair. He stroked, hoping to soothe away any lingering ugliness.

"I'm sorry."

Coy's apology caught Law off guard. "Why?"

He felt Coy shrug. "Because I can't stop leaning on you. I know I'll need to find a new way to cope. It's just that none of that shit my counselor suggested works for me. Sometimes I can't breathe at night. I don't want Jonah to know how fucked up I am."

Law's lips skimmed Coy's shoulder again. "You're not fucked up."

Coy snorted.

Law couldn't stop kissing the man's shoulder. "You're not. I'm fucked up. You're still trying." Law had given up years ago, but his heart kept beating, keeping a dead body and soul alive. Coy's soft skin made Law wish for things he'd never have. His lips moved to Coy's neck. "Don't stop showing up. Okay?"

Coy didn't respond right away. When he did, his voice sounded strained. "One of these nights, you won't be alone, and I'll have to stop."

Law held Coy tighter. "I'll always be alone."

"Why?"

The instant knot in Law's gut proved how unprepared he'd been for the question. "Why do you have nightmares?"

"You don't want to know that."

Law did, but he also didn't care to admit why no one would ever want him. "Get some sleep. I won't let anything happen to you."

He felt Coy nod. "I know."

At the conviction in Coy's tone, Law's eyes fell closed. Eventually, Coy would find someone else. He'd find a real man who would keep him safe. That guy would make love to Coy and soothe away his fears, ensuring he felt cherished. Law would go back to being alone. He wasn't sure it wouldn't kill him when that day came.

SIX

AFTER STRIPPING DOWN TO ONLY HIS JEANS, LAW slipped back into bed with Coy. He'd managed to sneak away without disturbing Coy long enough to assign duties for the day and find Coy the essentials for when he woke up—a toothbrush and whatnot. Law had been more than a little worried Coy would wake up while he was gone and leave before Law made it back. He didn't want to miss this. Watching Coy sleep was one of his favorite pastimes. Most people softened in their sleep, looking younger. Not Coy. His expression turned wicked—like being bad was his natural state. Law couldn't get enough.

As he settled down into his spot, Coy rolled his way. Law didn't hesitate to offer his chest as a pillow.

Coy's hand slid across Law's stomach. Law closed his eyes and savored the sensation. Years ago, he'd come to terms with spending his life alone, but human touch was something everyone needed. He'd been starved of that contact for a long time. Before he got to fully enjoy the moment, Coy shot up.

After bolting upright, Coy blinked at his surroundings before focusing on Law. His confused expression didn't clear.

"What time is it?"

"Ten."

Coy blinked a few more times. "In the morning?"

An unexpected smile snapped to Law's lips. "Yes."

"Why aren't you working?"

Law sat up, snagged Coy's waist, and rolled, leaving Coy no other choice but to lie back down. "I'm taking the day off."

"Seriously?" Obviously recognizing how disbelieving he sounded, Coy tried backpedaling. "I mean, you never miss work. Do you even take days off? I've never seen it."

"You're seeing it now," Law said with a chuckle.

Coy stroked the arm Law had wrapped around him. Law held tighter. "What made you decide to suddenly become a lay-about?"

"This," Law answered honestly.

Coy glanced over his shoulder. "Why? You don't even like me."

Law couldn't fight his eye roll. "You know that's not true." Even to his ears, Law sounded sad. There was no way Coy truly believed that.

He felt the fight drain from Coy. Coy relaxed into his hold.

"I can't believe I slept so late."

Just like last night, Law couldn't stop his lips from finding Coy's nape. "You needed the rest," Law said against Coy's skin. Chill bumps rose beneath his lips. God, he wished he couldn't feel. He couldn't stop. Law ran his knuckles down Coy's arm. His teeth scraped Coy's nape. It was out of his control. He heard Coy's breath catch. The goosebumps seemed to double. Coy made him feel powerful. He didn't want to lose this feeling. Law knew he couldn't keep it. That didn't stop him.

"You confuse me."

Coy's breathless tone was hot. "I know." He rolled away. "I'm sorry."

Coy reached behind him, blindly grabbing for Law. "I didn't say I wanted you to stop."

Even though he knew he should leave Coy in peace, Law molded against Coy's back again like he was meant to fit there. His lips found Coy's skin, incapable of being elsewhere. He palmed Coy's hip. Every breath Law took came harder than the last until he sounded like he'd raced to get there. With no input from his brain, Law's hand found its way inside Coy's workout shorts. Coy's back arched. Law's mouth opened over the side of Coy's neck. He sucked as his fingers closed around Coy's erection. The hunger was real. Law had never wished or wanted so hard in his life. He had one option—to pleasure Coy. Law had nothing else. He told himself this would be enough. After today, he'd give up this dream and let Coy find happiness. He'd stop confusing Coy and giving him hope. He'd let go.

Coy moved against Law's hand, unashamed and openly taking his pleasure. Moans vibrated from Coy's chest and slammed into Law's heart. Law shoved Coy's shorts lower, giving himself more freedom to work before reclaiming Coy's cock. He stroked. Coy reached over his head and held Law in place against his neck. Law didn't let up. He sucked and bit even as he pumped, bringing Coy closer to the edge. A fine sheen of sweat rose on Coy's skin. His muscles tensed. Law squeezed his eyes closed and committed every minute detail to memory. Coy's breaths left him, sounding like a shot. Law fought for air as if the pleasure was his. Coy's body jerked in his hold. A cry escaped him. Law held on, massaging Coy's dick even after the last drop of cum fell. He kissed the shell of Coy's ear, savoring the sound of Coy's ragged breathing.

"Thank you."

A sexy-sounding chuckle escaped Coy, caressing Law's ears. "For what? I'm pretty sure I'm the one who should be thanking you."

No. He shouldn't. One day, sooner rather than later, Coy would hate him for this moment. A moment he'd stolen something that didn't belong to him and never would. Coy would remember how Law gave him every reason to believe they'd be together, only to walk away.

"You give me more than you could ever know," Law confessed. He rolled from the bed before Coy responded. Law headed for the bathroom, avoiding his reflection as he wet a washcloth with warm water and grabbed a towel. He didn't need to look at himself to see the devastation. Law felt the wreckage. He kept his gaze locked on his hands and task as he cleaned Coy's skin and straightened Coy's clothes. This was the only time he'd get to show his love for Coy, and Law's heart knew it. That ridiculous organ begged Law to hang on to Coy, not let him slip away.

"I found you an unopened toothbrush while you were asleep. You can take a shower if you want and I'll take you home afterward."

Coy touched his arm. Law's gaze shot to Coy's without his brain's permission. The flush on Coy's cheeks made the blue of his eyes seem even lighter. Law's throat swelled. Coy looked trusting—like Law would never hurt him. Yet all Law ever did was hurt him. "Are you okay?"

Despite the pains in his chest, Law smiled. He brushed his knuckles down Coy's jaw because he had to touch him. "Yes. I just don't want you to take another cab." No one knew how much that lie cost him. He'd pretended to be okay his whole life. This one time, it was harder than all the others combined.

With a nod, Coy sat up. "I'll take a shower at Jonah's."

Law moved away, tossing the towel and washcloth in the laundry basket before retrieving Coy's shirt from the floor. He fought the urge to bring it to his nose before handing it Coy's way. Before Coy, Law hadn't realized a person's scent could be addicting. While Coy brushed his teeth, Law found a shirt and socks. Side by side, they readied to leave. It felt like the last time. In his heart, Law recognized he'd never get to hold Coy again. If Coy had another nightmare, he wouldn't call. On the drive to Jonah's, Law kept the radio turned off, savoring the final minutes of Coy. Without a single qualm, he held Coy's hand. Law knew—later—Coy would resent everything about this day, so he didn't deny himself. One more mistake wouldn't change anything. After parking in front of Jonah's, Law circled the truck and opened Coy's door. It would be the last time he got to show his love in some small way. He didn't want to miss out.

"Do you need a ride to work tonight?" Law asked over his shoulder as he headed for the porch.

"Jonah has been letting me use his car. I just didn't want to take it last night without him knowing," Coy said as he trailed behind him. When Law reached Jonah's front door, he turned. He didn't want to go. Coy stared at his feet, keeping his expression and feelings hidden.

"John's lawyer, Brad, asked me to lunch tomorrow." Coy looked nervous—like he didn't know how Law would react. He chewed his bottom lip as if he expected Law would explode. It made Law sad to think about how Coy had been treated in the past—how he'd been trained to always expect the worst of everyone. He imagined Coy half expected to get hit over such a confession.

"You should go." The words were fire lashing at Law's throat.

Coy flinched as if he had been hit. He looked away. "Oh." Coy swiped his palms on his shorts while looking in every direction except Law's. "Okay. If that's what you want."

A voice in Law's head screamed no. That wasn't what he wanted. Thankfully, his mouth showed common sense. "I've met Brad. He seems like a nice guy." Law swallowed. There was no sense in pretending they were real. "Besides, I can't give you the life you deserve. You're young. You should be with someone who can keep up with you."

Coy snorted. His laughing gaze swung Law's way. "You work more than anyone I've ever met. I can't keep up with *you*. Don't tell me this is about age," Coy said, showing a surge of bravery. "You of all people should know I'm closer to eighty at heart. Life killed my youth a long time ago."

A growl rose in Law's throat. "I'm not talking about age. Although that is off-putting. I mean, I'm old enough to be your dad."

To his surprise, a bright smile lit Coy's face. "I don't think you need to worry anyone will believe that."

Despite the situation, a soft chuckle escaped Law. His fingers found Coy's without thought. The moment they touched, Law brought Coy's hand to his mouth. His eyes slipped closed as Law kissed Coy's fingertips. He'd never felt anything like he did for Coy. That was why he had to be honest and set him free. Law's eyes opened. His heart shattered as he saw his feelings returned in Coy's stare. "You're the greatest person I know. That's why I want you to be happy, even though I know it won't be with me." He sucked in a deep breath and let the truth fly. "I'm impotent."

Coy's eyebrows drew together in a frown. "Okay. What does that have to do with anything?"

A shot of longing so intense it nearly brought Law to his knees hit Law in the gut. He knew, because Coy was an amazing person, Coy truly believed Law's impotence wouldn't matter. It would. It always did eventually. Law kissed Coy's fingers again and released him. "I love you." Law had no qualms with admitting as much. "Go to lunch with Brad. Be happy. I want that for you." No matter how much it killed him.

"Don't do that to me."

The deep betrayal in Coy's voice confused Law. "Do what?"

Coy's gorgeous eyes flashed with fire. "Don't tell me you love me and turn me away in the same sentence. That's cruel."

Everything about this was unfair. There was an invisible weight crushing Law's chest and throat. He held Coy's stare and inched closer. Coy didn't back down. He tilted his chin up, openly daring Law to make a move. Law's fingers brushed Coy's jaw. It happened with no thought. As long as Coy was within touching distance, Law would touch him. That was why he needed to stay away. He dipped his head and captured Coy's lips. It was the sweetest clinging of lips. Law's eyes stung. This life, it was hell. Law's entire being burned with desire and no amount of gut-wrenching want would make his body work right. He'd learned over the years how to bring himself to climax, but he'd never be able to make love to Coy. Coy might think that wasn't important, but— eventually—he'd miss having someone inside him. There would always be a part of him that would be restless and unfulfilled. Law couldn't do that to Coy because he hadn't lied. He loved Coy.

With his eyes squeezed shut, Law pulled away and pressed his forehead to Coy's. He held Coy's face between his hands while committing the moment to memory. For a little while, he'd gotten to pretend Coy could be his. Coy would never understand how huge of a gift he'd given Law by letting him dream. Coy would go to Brad. He would be happy, and Law would accept it. Law tore his hands away. His heart screamed so loud in denial, Law wondered if he'd go deaf. He jumped behind the wheel of his truck and drove away before he ruined Coy's life. Someday, Coy would recognize he'd narrowly escaped a hellish life. Unfortunately, Law already knew he'd narrowly missed out on heaven.

SEVEN

Coy couldn't stop swiping his palms on his jeans. If there was anyone who sucked more at being an adult than him, Coy had never met them. Green's Fighter Fuel wasn't a huge place. At least, the office area wasn't huge. The warehouse behind the office employed hundreds of locals. Coy wondered if he should apply for a job while he was here. Through a set of glass double doors, he spotted John sitting behind a desk. His huge frame made the oak piece look smaller than it should. Coy breathed a sigh of relief when John didn't glance up as he passed. Coy needed to talk to Brad and his nerves couldn't handle anything else until then. A young guy, close to Coy in age, looked Coy's way and then stepped into his path. His suit looked like it cost a fortune. His perfectly styled dark hair and condescending smile said he was worlds above Coy and knew it.

"Is there something I can help you with?"

Coy forced his hands to still before wiping them on his jeans again. "I'm looking for Brad Hollister."

Dark green eyes swept down Coy's body. Coy felt underdressed in his t-shirt, ripped jeans, and work boots. The guy's expression screamed Coy didn't belong. "Is he expecting you?" Something about the guy's sneer brought out Coy's long lost cockiness.

"Yes. We have a date." Coy let his smile turn wicked, leaving no room for doubt what type of date it would be. The man's expression changed. Coy swore the temperature in the room dropped by ten degrees.

"I see." He dropped a stack of files on a nearby desk. "In that case, let me show you the way."

Coy had a bad feeling he'd just stepped on some toes. He couldn't stop himself from eyeing the guy as he followed on his heels. Despite Brad's profession, Coy didn't think the man matched well with a perfectly pressed office worker. First of all, Brad was nice. This guy was not.

With a sharp perfunctory knock, he threw open a door. "Mr. Hollister. Your date has arrived."

Coy didn't miss the sneered emphasis on date. Still, Coy didn't stop smiling like they'd be besties. "Thank you..." He realized too late they hadn't been introduced.

"Thanks, Jake," Brad said, filling in the blank with a dismissive glance before his gaze moved Coy's way. His expression shifted from bland to sweet and welcoming in an instant. Jake already forgotten, Coy stepped into the room.

"Hey."

Brad brightened even more. "Hey. You're early."

"Yeah." Coy's face heated unexpectedly. "Sorry about that."

For a moment, Brad stared at Coy in silence. He looked happy to see Coy, and it was... nice. His eyes flashed with irritation as they slid Jake's way. "Thanks, Jake. I can take it from here."

Coy purposely didn't look Jake's way at Brad's admonishment. He knew it was petty, but people had looked down on him a lot the past year or so. He kind of liked making one person jealous, even if it was an unnecessary envy. Without a word, Jake shut the door with more force than needed.

Brad winced. "Sorry about that."

"No worries. I bring out the worst in some people."

A sexy-sounding chuckle escaped Brad. "Trust me. It's not you." Brad leaned back in his chair. His light green gaze swept over Coy, making Coy fight another blush. "You look gorgeous today." Before Coy could call him a liar, Brad motioned toward a nearby chair. "If you don't mind, I have to finish one last thing before we go."

"That's fine." Especially since Coy didn't intend to go anywhere with Brad. He sat and tried gathering his courage. Coy's knee bobbed up and down. He caught himself before he chewed his nails. Brad was gorgeous. Coy stared at the man's profile as he read something on his computer screen. It didn't surprise Coy in the least someone had challenged his right to be there. Brad probably had dozens of men fighting to be with him. He had a good job. Coy could already imagine his mom's face if he told her he was dating a lawyer. But in the end, Coy was in love with someone else. That wasn't fair to Brad.

"You're an amazing guy."

Brad looked his way and winked.

Coy took a deep breath. "You're just not my amazing guy." Brad's gaze slid his way once more and stayed. Coy talked faster as his nerves kicked in. In his experience, men didn't take rejection well. That was why he'd chosen to do this here. "I don't want to do anything to give you the wrong impression, or make you feel led on, but I also think you deserve for me to tell you in person I don't think we should have lunch today."

Brad's mouth lifted in one corner, obviously entertained by Coy's discomfort. "I won't say I'm not disappointed. It's not often I meet anyone like you. I don't know if you realize this, but you're unique."

To Coy's surprise, he found himself blushing again. Brad possessed an uncanny knack for flustering Coy. No one had ever called him unique. He never would've expected to be flattered by such an odd compliment, but it was Brad's tone. It couldn't have been more obvious that unique was what did it for him. "If I'd met you a year ago, you could've easily swept me off my feet." Coy made a helpless gesture.

"Now I have to win this stupid cowboy who doesn't know his worth. He already owns me."

"Ah. Lawson Yates," Brad said, leaning back in his chair. "Jonah warned me he might pose a problem. You know, as long as we've done business with Baker Ranch, I don't believe I've ever heard of Law dating anyone. Not that I keep up," he quickly tacked on.

"I'm aware," Coy said, trying to fight back the hopelessness of the situation.

Brad's chest expanded. After a second, he released a loud sigh. "Well, this sucks. I don't guess I could convince you to still go lunch with me anyhow, could I? The last thing I want is Jake gloating to my ex that you left before we even had our first date."

That explained a lot. "Jake is friends with your ex?"

"They're brothers, actually. It doesn't seem to matter Easton was the one who cheated. I'm still the bad guy somehow."

Ugh. Exes. They were the worst. "Well, technically, I'm single, so there's no reason Jake can't think we're dating. May I take you to lunch, Mr. Hollister?"

"Hmmm. You twisted my arm. Let's go." Brad pushed to his feet.

With the burden of Brad getting the wrong impression lifted from his shoulders, a real smile tugged at Coy's lips. "I have a feeling we could get in so much trouble together."

"We should," Brad said, steering him toward the door. "What sort of trouble would you like to stir up first? As long as I don't lose my license to practice, I'm up for anything."

As long as it didn't mean losing his shot at Law, Coy was too. "Let's start with lunch and go from there."

Brad's smile made everything seem brighter. "I like this plan."

Coy did too. Judging by how things had left off with Law, Coy might need all the new friends he could get. Otherwise, the rest of his life could be lonely as hell.

THE VINEYARD WAS quiet this time of year. Law liked walking the rows, enjoying the peace. Since the day he'd met Coy, there hadn't been a peaceful moment in Law's life. Today was no different. He ran through every second of his last morning with Coy, taking him home, and especially everything that had been said and done after he walked Coy to the door. Law scrubbed at his face. He'd needed that kiss. Yet his heart couldn't accept it would be the last one.

As he reached the end of the row, Law delved deeper into the trees surrounding the vineyard. He didn't want to see anyone today. Some days, his mind was too loud. Law worried if anyone got too close today, he'd turn into his mother. Sometimes, he could feel the rage building. Usually, it poured out in the form of scathing comments and sarcasm. With Coy gone, he wasn't sure what form the fury would take. Black energy pushed at his brain. Law stopped walking and tilted his chin to the sky. A scream rose in his throat. His hands curled into fists. A roar sounded in his mind. His phone buzzed. Law scrambled to dig his phone from his pocket. As he stared down at the device, a series of images appeared. Empty rooms. A large kitchen. Next up, a fenced-in backyard. Hardwood floors.

Coy: *My soon-to-be new home, I guess. I meant to send you pictures the other day, but it was full of workers.*

Law spent another minute looking through the images before responding.

Law: *Why do you seem less than thrilled? The place looks great.*

Coy: *It's the house John bought for Jonah when they were dating. I'm not sure I can afford the rent and I don't want to fail Jonah. He's the only person who believes I'm a semi-normal, functioning adult.*

Even though the rage had disappeared at the first sight of Coy's name, it had been replaced with a deep sense of loss. He might not be able to be who Coy needed, but Law could make sure he was always secure.

Law: *If you fall on hard times, just let me know. I can cover you.*

Coy: *That's nice. I'll keep your offer in mind. I won't take you up on it, but I appreciate you nonetheless. How's Belle?*

After moving to a nearby fallen tree, Law sat and focused all his attention on Coy.

Law: *I decided to put Rick in charge of her care. If I make her nervous, I won't force my attention on her. Do you need any help tonight? We're slow around here. I could come help you clean Ty's office again.*

Coy: *There's not much to do tonight after the way we scrubbed the place last time. Thanks for that again. I didn't realize all those animal cages would be such a pain.*

Law: *Anytime.* Law hesitated before adding, *Things aren't the same around here without you.*

Coy: *LOL! What? Is there no one else for you to torment?*

Law: *No one with your wit. It's unfair to fight an unarmed opponent.*

Coy: *I'm always only a text away.*

If only he could reach through a text and hold on to Coy.

Law: *The same goes for you. I'll always be here.*

Waiting. Law wouldn't add that last part, even though it was the truth. He feared it would always be true. For the rest of his life, Law would be right here, living a half-life and completely aware of what he'd missed. Yeah. He was in for a long, empty life without Coy.

"What's got you hiding out today?"

Law glanced over his shoulder. David headed his way. He waited to respond until David straddled the tree and sat. "How do you always find me?"

"You always go to the same places." David's voice was full of good humor. He was a nice person. Law truly believed God had been looking out for him when he'd stumbled into Baker Ranch as a kid.

"Comfort in familiarity, I suppose," Law said absently as he stared at nothing in the distance.

"Tyrone and I just had lunch at one of my restaurants. I saw Coy there." Law's ears perked at the mention of Coy's name, but he kept his gaze averted. David didn't take pity on him. "I don't think you're too late."

Law's gaze moved David's way at the comment without permission from his brain.

David flashed a knowing smile and didn't let up. "He was headed to look at Jonah's old house now that all the work is complete. I guess he plans to rent the place. But it hasn't happened yet. So, you know, you could still get your shit together, man up, and beg him to take mercy on you."

Law looked away. "I have no idea what you mean."

David scoffed. Law didn't blame him. Even to his ears, his denial sounded half-assed. "The world is filled with fools. Neither of us are on that list. Unless you plan on letting Coy get away."

"That's exactly what I plan."

After a brotherly pat to Law's shoulder, David stood. "I'm sure you have your reasons. I just hope they're damn good ones, because—judging by the way John and Jonah's lawyer was eyeing the guy at lunch—I'd say you don't have much time to change your mind. Brad won't wait for you to wise up before making his move."

Law flinched as the words hit their mark. Did he intend to let Coy move on with someone else? Yes, he planned to do just that. Did he think he would die from it? Also, yes. Law very much feared that the moment someone else touched Coy, he'd instantly transform into a dried husk and get carried away by the first strong wind. It didn't matter, as long as Coy was happy somewhere in the world. If he knew Coy was settled, Law could endure anything.

SPENDING the day with Brad turned out to be a lot better than Coy expected. Lunch had gone so well, Brad had taken off the rest of the day. After eating, they'd caught a movie, which was something Coy hadn't done in ages. The day had been nice and normal. Coy couldn't even remember the last time he'd considered a day normal. He'd also forgotten how to breathe easy until he'd realized halfway through dinner with Brad that he hadn't been forced to remind himself to take full breaths all day. No one had insulted him. He hadn't flinched away from anyone's touch. Coy understood now why Law wanted this life for him. The thing was, Law wanted this life for him. No one else loved him that much.

While relaxing on the window seat inside his assigned bedroom, Coy stared out the window at the pool. At least, he tried looking at the pool. The couple currently occupying a huge three-person lounge kept capturing his gaze instead. From three floors up, Coy couldn't make out any real details of John and Jonah's make-out session. That was the only thing keeping Coy from feeling like a voyeur. But he also didn't look away. They were in love. It was a healthy love too, unlike anything Coy had known in his life. Coy blinked rapidly at the sudden burning behind his eyes. Sometimes, other people seemed to have it so much easier than Coy. Almost everyone he knew managed to maintain real connections. Meanwhile, Coy was just lost.

An image of Law kissing his fingertips kept floating through Coy's mind. He curled his hand into a fist, trying to hang on to the phantom sensation of Law's lips. His gaze moved back to John and Jonah. It was hard to tell from this height, but he was almost certain they weren't actually fucking. No one looked unclothed. Nonetheless, they were making love, and that was exactly what he didn't know how to make Law understand. It wasn't that he hadn't thought things through. He'd done nothing but think about Law's confession. Coy knew he needed to be honest with himself. If there was any chance he could hurt Law down the road because he couldn't live with Law's impotence, Coy needed to admit it to himself now. Watching John and Jonah only reinforced his beliefs. Coy wasn't afraid. He was scared of a lot of things, but disappointment in Law wasn't one.

Coy dug out his phone and pulled up Law's number. He typed several texts and deleted each one. Nothing he said seemed adequate because Coy wasn't. He'd known for years he was missing something fundamental that made him worthy of a good man. Coy didn't possess powerful words. He couldn't call Law and convince him of anything. Coy tossed his phone aside with a growl. He scrubbed his fingers through his hair in frustration. His gaze automatically sought the couple below. What would Jonah do in his place? If John turned him away because of something neither of them could change, how would Jonah convince John to come back? Coy looked away, defeated. John was nothing like Law. It would take an act completely out of the box and over the top to floor him.

Coy stared at the wall, seeing nothing. A smile pulled at the corners of his mouth. Coy wasn't Jonah.

He couldn't picture Jonah humiliating himself for anyone. Coy was an expert at degradation. It wasn't possible for anyone to think less of him. So, really, he could do anything. Coy's smile grew. He would do anything.

EIGHT

THERE WAS A SPOT AT THE BACK OF THE STABLES. It was Law's spot. He could open the back door and sit at the threshold for hours, staring at the night sky. After more than thirty years, the view was still as amazing as it had been the first night Tim had taken him in. This place meant freedom. Always had. Always would. But tonight, nothing brought him peace.

The rest of the crew had a raging bonfire going. They'd busted out the booze and passed three sheets to the wind hours ago. Law wasn't much of a drinker, but they were fun to watch. Alcohol had been his mother's demon. Well, her first real vice had been love. She'd turned to drinking after falling for an older doctor. He'd been married with children, but that hadn't stopped her. She'd thought giving birth to his son would finally steal him from his family. Instead, he'd left her in the dust. In turn, she'd hated her son. To this day, Law knew her relief had to have been great at finding him gone. Law was the living reminder of her sins. Nobody knew how unfair he found life sometimes. It seemed, after surviving her, he should be allowed some happiness. Instead, he was forced to settled for peace. Tonight, even that emotion eluded him.

At a young age, he'd realized he was drawn to people's minds and not their bodies. While other teens had bragged about all the people they'd fucked, compared asses and breasts, Law found all of that uninteresting. He'd never considered himself gay. Nor was Law straight. In fact, he didn't think much about sex at all. Then he'd tried it and failed. After that horrible incident, all he'd thought about for a long time was sex and how he'd never be normal. Eventually, he'd settled into single life. Law had been determined to be happy with what he had. Tim had left him a lot of money when he'd passed and a stake in the land. He was set and could stay here forever, hiding from real life. The thing was, Law hadn't realized he was hiding, until Coy. Now, not only did he see how much he didn't have, he felt the lack everywhere he looked. As if his heart needed the punishment, his gaze slid David's way. He sat on the ground between Ty's knees. The man who'd stolen David's heart leaned forward in his chair, running his fingers through David's hair, massaging his scalp. David's blissful expression made Law's eyes burn. He wanted that. To sit by the fire, on the land he loved, savoring the touch of the person he loved most in the world. Law would always be right where he was now—alone. He swallowed. His throat felt like razor blades tore through his flesh. Was Coy with Brad right now? Law rubbed his chest, massaging the ache. He'd told him to go to Brad. Brad was a lawyer and had great friends. John would keep the guy in check, and—no doubt—Brad would always do everything within his power to keep Coy happy. That was what Law wanted. Wanting that life for Coy didn't make it hurt any less that it would never be with him. He recognized his loss.

A commotion near the edge of the barn had all eyes turned that way. From Law's vantage point, he couldn't see what had everyone's attention. Their drunken smiles brightened. Several people laughed.

Law found himself leaning forward, trying to catch a glimpse. Finally, the tallest man Law had ever seen stepped into view. From head to foot, he was covered in clown gear. No detail had been overlooked. Bright red, curly wig. Giant shoes. An outfit so bright it reflected the moonlight, making the guy look like he wore neon, glow-in-the-dark coveralls. He even had the big red nose and white stars painted around his eyes. He carried dozens of balloons. So many, Law expected the dude to get carried away like they did in the cartoons. All Law could do was stare, bemused, as he joined the partygoers.

"I'm here for Lawson Yates."

Every head turned his way. Horror overcame Law as David's already bright smile turned evil and he pointed at Law. "He's right there."

The clown turned and zeroed in on Law. His long stride and even longer shoes ate up the distance between them until he hovered over Law. Law stood. He didn't like being intimidated by anyone, especially a clown.

"Lawson Yates?" His disgruntled tone had Law biting back a nervous laugh.

"Yeah."

"I'm Binky, the singing clown. These are for you," he said, handing the dozens of balloons to Law. "Somebody is a fool over you," Binky said, honking a horn in his pocket. That was all the warning Law got before Binky belted out a loud song. Law jumped as the squeaky voice boomed through the air. All he could do was watch in mesmerized horror as he danced while singing off key. He prayed for it to stop. All eyes were on him. People were moving closer and pulling out their phones to capture video proof of his humiliation. For real, he'd never live this down. Before the song ended, a woman appeared. She was dressed like a blond buxom beauty from the fifties. David pointed at Law again. Heat burned Law's cheeks. He had no idea what was happening to his life. The woman handed him what had to be three dozen roses. He was too mortified to count. She calmly waited until the clown finished his dance. After he received a round of thunderous applause, the woman took over. Before he could react, she leapt forward and kissed his cheek. "Coy says he loves you, but he'll make a scene all night if you don't man up."

Just the mention of Coy's name had Law smiling. Even when the woman began singing with drunken catcalls in the background, all Law could do was shake his head and smile. Coy had done this? This was the most ridiculous thing he'd ever witnessed. There were already three more impersonators lined up to take their turn. It was like they'd carpooled. All Law had to do was take a step back and close the door. He could shut himself away inside the barn and be done with this sideshow. Law couldn't move because Coy had done this.

Rick sidled closer. "Damn, man. You must have shown someone a real good time. I ain't never seen nothing like this."

Law was without words.

The next performer took over. "Coy says there's only one way to make this stop."

From the corner of his eye, Law saw Rick's head whip around. "Dude. All this is from Coy? Are you joking? I never would've guessed. I mean, I thought... well, you know, that you were straight or whatever. Not that it matters. Plus, you don't even like Coy. Why would he think that you do?"

Suddenly, everything made sense. This wasn't about embarrassing Law. Coy was the one who looked like a fool in the equation. He looked like a desperate stalker, and it was a purposeful act. Law's throat swelled. He dropped his chin and stared at his feet. His eyes burned. Honest to god, he'd never met anyone like Coy. Someone willing to embarrass themselves to prove they couldn't be budged. Coy deserved better. Unless Law did something drastic, everyone would think Coy was crazy and pathetic. Law passed the balloons and roses to Rick and pulled out his phone. He ran for the nearby picnic table and climbed on top, calling Coy on FaceTime as he went. The moment Coy's image appeared on the phone, Law turned his back to the chaos, where Coy could see the carnage he'd caused. The sight of Coy's gorgeous smile and the hair he loved running his fingers through made Law almost forget his reason for calling.

Law yelled so everyone could hear, "Everyone else is here. Where are you?"

A sexy chuckle came through the line, making Law's smile grow. "You know why. Are you having fun?"

"Not as much as I would be if you were here. Everyone misses you, especially me." Law looked behind and yelled over the mayhem, "Doesn't everyone miss Coy?"

At a minimum, David and Tyrone yelled back their agreement.

"See?" Law said. As he stared at Coy, Law knew he was making the right choice. If there was ever anyone worth a risk, it was Coy. Law looked behind him for support again. "Tell the man I love to get his ass here before I think of a way to get even for this surprise of his."

"Get here," David yelled, making Law proud.

When he looked back at the phone, Coy held his phone close to where he had his chin resting on his arm. With his bottom lip between his teeth, Coy looked like he was trying not to smile. Coy cleared his throat. When he spoke, he sounded like it hurt to speak. "I love you."

Law leapt down the opposite side of the table and moved away from the noise. "I love you too. Why aren't you headed for that car Jonah is loaning you?"

"I wasn't sure if you were serious."

"I wouldn't ask if I didn't want you. Seriously, Coy. Come see me."

"Okay." Coy still didn't sound convinced. "I'll be there soon."

The weight was back on Law's chest. He'd never been this scared of anything. "I'll be waiting." Law disconnected the call. He glanced behind him. Rick still held the balloons and flowers. Now he also wore a crown and danced along with some woman playing a guitar. It seemed he'd not only taken Law's place, but Rick enjoyed the position. Law stole the opportunity to duck beneath the fence and cut through the field to the house, escaping without notice. He needed to catch Coy before he went to the stables. It was well past time they talked.

COY'S stomach shook with nervousness. The drive to Law's felt like a trip to judgment day. Tonight would make or break them. Coy recognized he'd only get this one chance. As soon as the front porch came into view, Coy spotted Law waiting. The shaking stopped. Everything went still. Law always had that effect on him. Rather than pulling around the house and into the garage, Coy turned into the driveway and parked by the front stairs. Law was immediately at his door, opening it.

"Hey."

Law helped him from the car like he couldn't do it himself. "Hey." Law looked nervous too. "I figured I'd meet you here, so we can talk before joining the party."

"Okay." The shaking was back. It was never good when someone wanted to talk.

After closing the door, Law crowded Coy against the car. "First, I need something else from you." Law touched his lips to Coy's. Coy's hands found Law's waist. The instant he touched Law, Law shuffled closer. He nibbled Coy's bottom lip and teased open Coy's mouth. Love overwhelmed Coy as their tongues met. He felt so much for Law, Coy didn't know how to contain his emotions. Law held Coy's face between his hands. His thumbs caressed Coy's cheeks as he explored Coy's mouth. For a moment, he lightly sucked Coy's bottom lip before pulling away. Coy wondered if he would melt into a puddle on the ground.

Law linked fingers with Coy and led him inside. He didn't slow on the way to his bedroom. After shutting them inside, Law urged Coy to sit on the bed. His silence was beginning to unnerve Coy. The feeling doubled when Law didn't join him on the bed. Coy tried focusing on other details to busy his mind. Law was so damn sexy. Years of hard labor had hardened his body into perfection. He wore a black and white open flannel over a white t-shirt. Both articles of clothing strained against his muscles. The soft-looking t-shirt clung to his washboard abs. His jeans were a little baggy everywhere but the thighs. Coy's palms itched to touch him. The way Law paced from his oak dresser to the open bathroom door and back again didn't give Coy much hope Law would let him touch him.

Coy ran his palms across Law's microfiber comforter, stroking the fabric and trying to soothe his frayed nerves. "Do you plan to talk to me?"

"Just gathering my thoughts," Law said, as if relentless pacing was how he began every conversation. Finally, Law faced him. His defeated expression didn't inspire confidence. "All I can think about is how much I'm stealing from you."

Coy felt his face screw up in confusion. He couldn't control it. "What are you stealing from me?"

"A normal, healthy life for starts."

No matter how hard he tried, Coy couldn't wrap his brain around Law's thought process. "How do you figure? I mean, I think you should expound so I can follow."

"I want everything with you, Coy," Law said—like the words came from his soul. "I love you. For almost a year, we've lived under the same roof. Most nights, we've shared the same bed. I don't want you at Jonah's. You're supposed to be here, with me, and in my bed. I want everyone to know you're mine. Whenever you're ready, I'd love to marry you." Fuck. Coy had nothing, or too much to say. He hadn't decided which. Thankfully, Law kept talking, so he didn't have to figure it out. "But I won't ever be able to make love to you and that breaks me. I don't know how to tie you to that life."

Law's explanation chafed. Coy fought not to roll his eyes. "You have some odd ideas about sex. There's more than one way to make love."

Law swiped his hand through the air, obviously frustrated. "I know that. You don't understand. How long do you think it'll be before you're bored?"

Coy shrugged. "How long does it take for anyone to get bored in any relationship? Maybe seven years like some people claim, or maybe it's never. That doesn't mean you give up. I don't understand why this is any different. Is it because you think I'm not worth it or do you just think that little of me and my ability to stay loyal?"

Law pulled a face that screamed disbelief. "Are you serious? You're perfect. I'm the problem. This is... ugh. I don't know how to make you understand." He made another helpless gesture. His arms fell to his sides. The fight seemed to drain from Law. "I'm scared. It terrifies me that you might only think you can handle this, but when the time comes, you'll feel different. That you'll be turned off or think that I'm less of a man."

Those were all valid feelings for a man in Law's position. Coy shoved his hands under his thighs so Law wouldn't see them shake. If Law could be brave and share his darkest fears and secrets, Coy would too. "Do you know why I have nightmares?" Coy didn't wait for Law to ask. He was too afraid he'd back down if he waited to speak. "It's because King used to rape me. A lot." Law's closed expression almost made Coy stop talking, but he couldn't. Law needed to understand. "When he'd drained all the fight from me, and it wasn't fun for him anymore, he started bringing his friends home to join." Coy's voice shook. He bit his bottom lip to calm the shaking and cleared his throat before continuing. "There's nothing that could ever make me think you're less than a man. I've seen half men. You're nothing like them." Coy swallowed the bitterness the way he always did. "You're not the only one who's terrified."

"It's medical," Law said fast like hot-waxing a cut. He motioned toward the lower half of his body as if Coy didn't know what he meant. "A severe lower body injury that hinders the flow of blood. I haven't lost any feeling. I can still come for you. It's just that I won't get hard. There are a few surgeries I haven't tried, but they're drastic." Now Law was the one clearing his throat. Coy carefully kept his expression blank. He needed Law to keep talking. This was the time to tell it all. "The woman who gave birth to me was a horrible person. Naturally, she also had terrible taste in men. Every time she'd meet someone new, things would get better—like she wanted them to think we were perfect so he'd keep us. Inevitably, things would go to shit, because the men she chose were usually married. This time, though, her hopes were higher than ever. The guy was rich, single, and by all appearances, a nice person. Things actually looked a little hopeful. Then, his birthday rolled around, and she bought him a set of golf clubs. They were expensive too. I know because I had to eat peanut butter crackers, only one a day, for two weeks to pay for his gift. We were making sacrifices for the future was what she kept reminding me when I'd say I was hungry. Anyhow, she'd put a bright blue bow on the clubs and baked a cake. It was more than she'd ever done for me. Ten minutes before he was supposed to be there, the phone rang. She took the call in her room, and when she came out, there was an odd calm about her. She looked at me and said, 'I hate you. You always ruin everything.' I tried running for the door because I knew that tone. Before I made it outside, she grabbed the closest club and hit me across the back of the knees. Once I was down, she didn't stop. I was already weak from barely eating for two weeks. It was probably the closest she ever came to killing me. There were many times I wished she had, because she ruined my life that day. All because some guy dumped her, and she was still stuck with me."

Coy swiped at his face. He hated crying, and he knew Law wouldn't appreciate his tears, but he couldn't take it. Coy knew what it was like to be defenseless. At least he'd been an adult. Picturing Law as a tiny, half-starved kid, enduring something so horrible at the hands of someone who should've always protected him was choking. He wished a woman he'd never met dead in that moment.

Law touched Coy's chin, forcing him to look at him. "Don't do that," Law said, brushing away Coy's tears. "That means her ugliness touched you. I can't let that happen."

"I love you. These are tears of rage."

Law's instant smile made the confession worthwhile. He inched closer, crowding Coy's space until Coy tumbled onto his back. Law straddled Coy's body. His wicked expression made Coy's mouth water. "I love you too." A shiver of delight ran through Coy at the admission. "More than that, I trust you." Coy's heart melted. "With everything. I've never let anyone else so close."

Coy didn't miss his chance to push for more. He cupped Law's face, drawing him closer. "Then you should make love to me. No shame. I want to see you come unglued."

Law sat back on his heels and stripped off his flannel and t-shirt. Coy's heart beat faster. That fear he'd mentioned earlier came calling. He knew Law wouldn't hurt him. Some cuts scarred deep. As if Law felt his fear, he rolled to the side, freeing Coy.

"I'm at your mercy, as always."

Fear turned to hunger. Coy rolled onto his knees. As he straddled Law's body, Law's expression turned heated. Coy couldn't lie to himself—he felt out of his element—but all he needed was the way Law looked at him to know he was turned on. The world was at Coy's fingertips. He didn't know where to start. Coy stroked Law's chest before running his hands down Law's torso. His mouth watered. He needed to taste him. Coy moved slow, dragging out the anticipation before capturing Law's mouth. He felt Law shudder beneath him. Heard his breath catch. Coy's cock twitched, trying to climb from his jeans. After only the slightest brushing of tongues, Coy nipped at Law's bottom lip and moved to nibbling on his neck.

Law shifted beneath him as if he fought to stay still. A smothered whimper escaped Law as Coy moved lower and scraped Law's nipple with his teeth. Coy reached for the button on Law's jeans. Law tensed.

Coy made a shushing sound against Law's chest. "Trust me." He said the words quietly, knowing Law could feel them. Law's muscles relaxed. Coy popped the button. He slid the zipper down as he shifted lower, kissing Law's stomach. Another stifled sound came from Law. Coy fought a smile as he licked Law's abs. With his weight balanced on his knees and his lips pressed to Law's skin, Coy urged Law to lift his hips so he could peel off the remainder of his clothes. Coy never stopped kissing some part of Law throughout the process. He didn't want Law to think. No doubt Law would needlessly fear the worst. The way Coy's dick leaked, soaking his underwear, proved Law wrong. It seemed love was the ultimate aphrodisiac. Coy had never wanted anyone more.

Law was semi-erect. As he'd warned, Law wasn't hard enough for penetration. But as Coy promised, it didn't matter. The way Law reacted to every touch and his cock dripped pre-cum; those things told the real story. Law wanted Coy. The instant Coy had Law bared, he didn't waste time. He opened his mouth over Law's dick and swallowed. Law's hips left the bed. His fingers found Coy's hair. A cry filled the air. Coy's erection begged for attention. He ignored the growing irritation of his clothes and sucked.

"Damn, Coy."

Coy clawed at the comforter, seeking purchase at the sound of his name on Law's lips in the perfect tone. All the times he'd fantasized didn't come close to reality.

Law held Coy's hair and openly sought his pleasure. Coy felt like he could take over the world. Law made him feel special—like he gave the man something no one else ever had. It was addicting. He didn't want to stop, but he also needed to feel Law's body beneath him as they moved together toward release. Even though he knew Law would give him forever, he wanted all the sensations he could get right now. He needed to prove they were beautiful and weren't missing anything. When Coy pulled away, Law's chest heaved and his eyes screamed murder. Coy suppressed an evil grin as he stripped.

Law's expression changed, going from ready to explode to needy in an instant. He caressed every place he could reach as Coy fought his way out of his clothes. The instant he was nude, Coy found himself on his back and covered with over six feet of muscle. Law kissed him hard and deep. His hips rolled, causing a delicious friction between them. Coy sucked in a gasp. The sound turned into a moan as Law reached between them and palmed their cocks. Law kissed and bit, leaving Coy breathless as the pressure built. Coy tore at Law's skin, trying to get closer. He was half insane with want. The sensation of Law's dick against his was a connection he couldn't describe. They were meant to be together. Coy felt it in his soul. Together, neither of them needed to live in fear. All the things that made them undesirable to everyone else made them beautiful together.

Pressure built, climbing up Coy's shaft and making him crazed. He bit Law's bottom lip and then sucked it in apology. Law growled. The sound hit Coy in the gut and sent him over the edge. He dug his heels into the bed and his short fingernails into Law's back as cum coated the space between them. Law threw his head back. His features hardened and strained. Coy couldn't look away. The cry Law released as he came seared itself on Coy's brain. In that moment, he knew he'd never be satisfied with anyone else. Wherever this man was, Coy would be there too. Law was his.

DESPITE HIS FIGHT TO get enough air, Law couldn't stop kissing Coy. Coy was so fucking beautiful, especially inside. This hadn't been faked. Coy wanted him exactly as he was—no illusions. The hope filling Law made him worry he'd explode. Not once had he allowed himself to dream. He couldn't let Coy get away. There was no length too far for Law. He would do anything to keep Coy.

"I love you."

Law's throat swelled at Coy's whispered words. How could one person give him so much and still be the first one to talk about love afterwards? Law kissed Coy's cheek. "I love you too." Even Law heard the quiver in his voice. Coy rocked him to his soul.

A loving caress smoothed down his back as Coy pressed his lips to the corner of Law's mouth. He had so much to say. His tongue wouldn't work.

"I think we need a shower." Coy's body shook with laughter as he made the claim. His open happiness was sexy. Law stared down at him, uncaring of the mess between them. All he wanted was to hold on to the moment. Almost a year ago, Coy had looked so different. Between the bruises and unhappiness, Coy had looked like a different person. Law had wanted to take away his pain. He'd never expected it to happen this way. Coy's earlier confessions about his life with King slammed into his mind again. Pure rage filled him. If King wasn't already dead, Law would happily kill him. He would keep Coy safe. As long as he lived, no one would touch Coy again. Law gathered Coy closer, spreading the mess even more. Coy shook harder. His laughter made even Law's heart smile.

"I don't want to share you."

A loud snort sounded against Law's ear. "You don't want to share me with the shower? You know we could take one together, right?"

Yes. He liked this plan. "I meant I don't want to share with anyone partying behind the stables. A shower sounds amazing. I especially like the idea of making you all slippery with soap." Once the idea took hold, Law wasted no time shuffling Coy into the shower. Even though Law's bathroom was huge, and the shower fit the room, Law refused to give Coy any space. With several shower heads hitting them from different directions, Law held Coy against his chest. He kept kissing Coy's ear, trying to appease his heart. "I don't want you to go back to Jonah's."

Coy stroked his waist. "David might have something to say about me staying here, since I'm no longer working for him."

"Actually, the house is half mine, so I don't think David would care."

Coy leaned back to meet his stare. "Seriously?"

Law nodded. "Tim left it to us fifty-fifty. He also left me a stake in the land along with some other stuff. David could've contested the will. Anyone else would have, but David said if Tim hadn't left it to me, he would've given it to me, because I'm every bit as much Tim's son as he is. We don't talk about it." Law shrugged. "We're family, though."

Coy went back to resting his cheek against Law's chest. "I guess that explains why you work so hard around here. You have as much to lose as David if anything fails."

"There's that," Law agreed. "Also, I don't have anything else."

"You have me." Coy punctuated the claim by kissing Law's chest.

A swell of happiness grew inside Law. "Does that mean you'll stay?"

"If that's what you want, yes."

Law couldn't hold back the tidal wave of elation. In a flash, he had Coy against the wall, attacking his mouth, and touching every place he could reach. He didn't know how to explain how it felt to suddenly have a future he'd lost hope in years ago. Law believed in Coy. He trusted him with everything. For the first time in his life, he knew someone loved him more than they loved themselves. Law would never let Coy regret it.

Coy's chuckle vibrated against Law's lips, making him smile. "I thought the point of this shower was to get clean. You're dangerously close to getting dirty." The final word came out sounding breathless as Law skimmed Coy's ass crack with his fingertips.

"This place never runs out of hot water. I have faith in my ability to get you dirty and clean in the same shower." Damn, Coy brought a side out in him Law had never seen. He'd always tried his damnedest be savage in every aspect of his life to make up for everything he lacked. Coy made him want to stay right here, doing exactly this and nothing else for the rest of his life. With his chin tilted up and holding Law's gaze, there was so much trust in Coy's expression. He left Law humbled. Coy also made him hot. The guy was sexy as hell. He lifted Coy's knee and held it to his hip as he shuffled even closer. His stomach muscles clenched with need. "You're beautiful."

"You are too."

An evil grin stretched Law's lips at Coy's breathless tone. "I have so many plans for you."

"Lawwwwwwww, where are you?"

Law's eyes fell closed in denial. All he wanted was time with Coy.

"What in the world?" Coy said, trying to see around him, as if someone had burst into the room.

"It's the intercom on the phone."

"Everyone is here, LawSON." Great. Rick sounded beyond plastered. "Some of those performance people decided to stay. The chick with the guitar and a couple of guys. Oh, and the clown. Dude, the clown is a trip, man. Grab Coy and get down here. Lawsonnnnnn."

Law dropped his forehead to Coy's shoulder. Coy held his head between his hands. His laughter filled the shower, bouncing off the walls. Damn, Law loved that sound. He lifted his head and met Coy's gaze. "Later," he promised, never meaning anything more.

Coy nodded. "Agreed."

With a growl, Law killed the water and grabbed a towel. He dried Coy with more enthusiasm than necessary. It was a little mean to leave Coy panting the way he did, but he would fix it later. Until then, he wanted Coy anticipating. They tossed each other heated glances as they dressed. Twice, Law stole kisses because he couldn't resist. Hand in hand, they cut through the field to the stables. They could hear the music and laughter long before anyone came into sight. A round of cheers went up as they reached the bonfire. Coy smiled and greeted people. Law couldn't look at anyone else. Someone found them lawn chairs. Law didn't pay attention to who. It seemed no sooner than they got settled, the entire party fell silent. All music stopped. It was so quiet, the horses could be heard moving around in their stalls.

David stood. "Now that everyone is finally here, I can move on to the reason I called you all here tonight." A round of laughter went up since David hadn't called anyone together. The party had been a spur-of-the-moment idea. David turned in a circle, eyeing his captive audience. "Everyone here is a huge part of my life. You're like family. That's why I couldn't do this without including everyone." Even Ty looked as confused as Law felt. Although David was accustomed to giving speeches, since he sat on the board of several charities, he didn't tend to make himself the center of attention at home. Everything became clear as David moved to Ty's side and dropped to one knee. "Tyrone Perry, you are the most amazing man on the planet. It would make my lifetime if you agreed to be my husband."

Ty looked shell-shocked. Law found himself watching Coy instead. At one time, he'd dated Ty. Law needed to know if Coy still felt anything for the too-sexy veterinarian. Coy was smiling hard—like he couldn't be happier for the couple. A round of cheers went up, telling Law he'd missed Ty saying yes. He still couldn't look away from Coy. Coy's gaze slid his way. Their gazes met. Coy's expression softened—like he was staring at the love of his life. Law fought the sudden sting behind his eyes. The tightening in his throat made it harder to breathe. In that moment, he saw the truth. He had nothing to fear because Coy felt exactly the same as Law. This was the love he'd waited for his entire life. They were in this together, for the long haul.

"I love you," Law mouthed, because he couldn't stop telling Coy every second how much he mattered.

Coy touched his cheek and lured him closer until their lips met. Law's heart skipped a beat. Life had never looked brighter.

***

KISSING LAW HAD BEEN out of Coy's control. Law had been watching him in that intense way that always left Coy breathless. It didn't take much after the way Law tried burning him alive in the shower, only to leave him wanting. With Law's lips clinging to his, Coy fought the urge to climb into Law's lap and make him very happy. After months of craving Law, Coy didn't have any patience left.

"David finished his announcement," Coy reminded him, keeping voice low. "You should steal me away."

Law kissed him again. A growl vibrated against his lips. "If we go back to the house, we'll probably have to listen to Rick screaming at us through the intercom the rest of the night."

Coy winced. There was nothing sexy about Rick's voice. "That's true. I guess we'll have to be sociable." He started to lean away, hoping some distance would cool his body. Before he settled in, Coy found himself on his feet and headed toward the stables. No one tried stopping them. In fact, somehow, Law managed to move so quickly and silently no one looked their way. They slipped through the open back door. Law headed toward the ladder that led to the hay loft slash land manager's office. He urged Coy up the ladder, crowding Coy's space the whole way. Coy couldn't stop smiling. He'd never been happier. The moment they reached the loft, Law kicked the hatch closed and slid the slide lock in place, ensuring no one could interrupt them. His mouth found Coy's before Coy had time to gather his bearings.

Law's hands found Coy's ass. He lifted, leaving Coy no other choice but to wrap his legs around Law's waist. He held on as Law grabbed a horse blanket and tossed it on top of the hay before easing Coy down on top. There was nothing comfortable about it, but he didn't care. He was there with Law. No amount of stabbing little straws or itchy blankets could penetrate his high, especially while Law kissed a path down his body. Coy blindly massaged every part of Law's body he could reach. Heavy panting filled the otherwise silent loft. He moved and lifted at Law's every silent command until they were both bare.

"I love you," Law whispered, sounding winded. "I'm sorry. I can't seem to stop saying it."

"Don't apologize. I love you too." Law's teeth scraped Coy's nipple. Coy's hips rose, seeking Law. His every movement was mindless. He wanted Law. Nothing else mattered.

"Jesus," Law breathed. "You're so hot. Everything you do sets me on fire. I'll never be able to do paperwork in here again without touching myself."

The image Law painted with his words had Coy's cock dripping. He wanted to watch Law pleasuring himself. "I'll come with you. You can give me a show." The final word came out on a gasp as Law's mouth surrounded his erection. He sucked, forcing Coy to cling to the hay like it was his sanity. His hips rolled. He had no pride. A wet finger slipped inside him. Incoherent words left Coy. Even he didn't know what he said. Law toyed with Coy's asshole as he licked and sucked. The ability to think abandoned Coy. All he could do was feel and Law made him feel everything. Pleasure. Loved. Coy felt like there was no one else on the planet but them. He'd never been cherished before Law. As the pressure built and ecstasy rocked him to his core, Coy accepted the truth. Not only was Law the only person he'd really loved, no one else would ever do. This man was everything. At times, he'd felt like Coy's enemy, but mostly, he was Coy's soul. That was something he couldn't live without.

NINE

STANDING ON THE FRONT STEPS OF COY'S mother's house, Coy watched Law fidget nervously with the gold gift box he held. Coy's heart swelled with pride. He couldn't love Law more.

"How do I look?"

Coy eyed Law at the question. He stifled a laugh as he smoothed out the man's white button-down denim woven shirt and straightened his cowboy hat. "Like a very sexy, dark chocolate cowboy who's ready to get some dollar bills stuffed in his G-string." Coy lost the battle against his laughter when Law's face screwed up in confusion.

"What?"

"It's the present," Coy explained. "The glitter from the gift box is all over you."

Law glanced down at himself. "Shit." He looked so miserable, Coy's heart melted.

He cupped Law's face, forcing him to hold Coy's stare. "Oh, baby. It's okay. I promise she'll love you, because I do."

"I don't know how to act around moms."

Coy fought the urge to kiss Law's nose. He loved this man so much, he couldn't contain it sometimes. Still, Law needed some teasing. "How do you treat all women your age?"

Law blinked. "I'm sorry."

"Technically, she's a year younger than you, though."

"The fuck you say."

"Damn, language, boys."

They spun at the sound of Coy's mom's voice. "Mom," Coy called, rushing to hug her.

At the same time, Law fell into a muttering mess. "Sorry. I mean, excuse me. I wasn't trying to be rude. You sneaked up on me. Well, it's your house, so I guess that's not true. I didn't know you were standing there. Here," he said, holding out the box to her.

His mom didn't reach for it right away. With her arm wrapped around Coy's waist, she shook her head. "You're right, Coy. He's adorable. Do you have a bachelorette party scheduled after this or did you get all glammed up for me?" she asked as she accepted the gift.

Law's shoulders seemed to fall another inch.

"I'm only messing with you. Where do you think my son got his evil streak? Certainly not from his nonexistent father." It was a speech Coy had heard many times. "Come here," she said, holding out her arms and wiggling her fingers in excitement. "I've been waiting to hug you forever. Gimme, Gimme."

The tension visibly drained from Law as he stepped into her hold. "It's nice to finally meet you, Sophie."

"Please, call me Mom," she said, squeezing him hard before backing away. "After all, in a few months, you'll be my son too."

Coy took a deep breath at the reminder. He wasn't nervous. It was more that he was too excited to breathe properly. From Law's first mention of marriage three months ago, they'd talked on occasion about a big wedding, and half-ass made plans for a wedding around Valentine's Day. In truth, it hadn't seemed that important, since they spent every second together. Between Coy returning to his job on the ranch and Law joining him each night to clean the clinic, they were always right on top of each other. Getting married was just one more step that wouldn't really change anything about them. Then, David and Ty got married. Their wedding changed everything. Coy wanted that. He wanted Law's last name and that piece of paper that meant nothing and everything. While David and Ty shared their first kiss as a married couple, Law and Coy had looked at each other at the same time, and a silent conversation passed between them. It was their turn.

"Actually," Coy said, seeing his chance at his mom's reminder. "We have something to tell you."

Sophie eyed them, looking wary as Coy reached for Law's hand. "Is everything okay? You didn't call off the wedding, did you? I mean, marriage isn't for everyone, but you two seem so happy."

"Don't be mad." Coy chewed his bottom lip.

"Whatever it is, you know I have your back," Sophie assured him.

He knew that, but she would be mad, of that he was sure. Law squeezed his hand, lending Coy strength. Coy took a breath and dropped their news. "We've decided to cancel the wedding."

"The fuck you say," Sophie spat, sounding exactly as Law had earlier. "I was supposed to be the hottest mom at this shindig."

"You would've been the only mom there," Coy reminded her. Her blue eyes that looked so much like his narrowed, and Coy scrambled to fix his mistake. "But you still would've been the hottest one, obviously."

His mom gave him a sharp nod before swishing her long, blonde curls over her shoulder. "Damn, right? I'm only forty-two. I'm not too old to rock a great mother-of-the-groom dress."

"Fuck," Law muttered at the reminder of Sophie's age.

Coy swiped his fingers over his mouth, trying to wipe away his smile. "Open the gift, Mom. I know we screwed you out of the wedding you wanted, so we thought we'd share our time with you instead."

Her eyebrows rose. "What?" She lifted the lid from the gift box that shed glitter like it waited for someone to make it rain. He made a mental note not to ask Rick to pick him up anything from the store again. Sophie peeked inside. "Is this seriously a ticket to join you on a cruise?"

Coy nodded, but Law did the explaining. "You'd have your own cabin and everything," Law assured her. "There's supposed to be a lot of fun things to do. We really just..." Law shrugged and tried again. Coy rubbed his back as Law spoke for the both of them. "Neither of us have many people in our lives. We didn't want to wait any longer to share what little family we have with each other. Coy and I also felt like a wedding wasn't the way to go for us. Instead, we'd like to spend a few weeks enjoying our new family dynamic."

Coy could tell Law had won Coy's mom. He decided to push her over the line and fully into Law's court.

"Plus, this way, you can rock a bikini instead of a dress and be the hottest mom on the ship."

She nodded, looking thoughtful. "This is all true." Her eyes appeared to snap back into focus. A smile slowly spread across her face. Coy knew his mom. He tensed, readying himself for the explosion. A piercing squeal escaped her as her feet left the ground and she launched herself at them. She jumped up and down while trying to hug them. Coy feared Law might lose an eye. Their gazes met. The smile stretching Coy's lips matched the one Law wore. A silent conversation passed between them. They'd wait until she was on the ship to break the rest of their news. His mom didn't like anything making her feel old or left out. That was why they'd booked her a cabin in an area meant for singles. Maybe she'd meet someone fun. She'd eat someone nice for breakfast, but a good time was up her alley. Once she was chilled and had a few drinks in her, then Coy would tell her they'd already gotten married. Then, if she still wanted to kill him, he'd let Ty talk her down, and he'd sneak away with Law. After all, all Law had to do was cash in his senior citizen discount, and boom, they could be alone. He liked the bright future they had in store.

Keep an eye out for the next book in the series, *Sugar Port*.

PLEASE CONSIDER LEAVING a review at the retailer where this book was purchased. Reviews really help with a book's visibility, which ensures I can continue writing. Thank you, Charity.

ABOUT THE AUTHOR

Charity Parkerson is an award winning and multi-published author with several companies. Born with no filter from her brain to her mouth, she decided to take this odd quirk and insert it in her characters.

*Eight-time Readers' Favorite Award Winner

*2015 Passionate Plume Award Finalist

*2013 Reviewers' Choice Award Winner

*2012 ARRA Finalist for Favorite Paranormal Romance

*Five-time winner of The Mistress of the Darkpath

Connect with her online:

--Join my street team: facebook.com/TeamCharityParkerson

--Sign up for my newsletter: http://bit.ly/CharityNews

--Website: charityparkerson.com

--Facebook: facebook.com/authorCharityParkerson

facebook.com/TheMenofSin

--Twitter: twitter.com/CharityParkerso

www.ingramcontent.com/pod-product-compliance
Lightning Source LLC
Chambersburg PA
CBHW060229180626
46813CB00007B/3014